smiling at grief
in a house in a forest
where life grows

smiling at grief
in a house in a forest
where life grows

Jan Fortune

LIQUORICE FISH BOOKS

Published by Liquorice Fish Books, an imprint of Cinnamon Press
www.cinnamonpress.com

The right of Jan Fortune to be identified as author of this work has been asserted by her in accordance with the Copyright, Designs and Patent Act, 1988. © 2024, Jan Fortune.
Print Edition ISBN : 978-1-911540-25-0

British Library Cataloguing in Publication Data. A CIP record for this book can be obtained from the British Library.

Designed and typeset in Adobe Garamond Pro and Bodini Book by Cinnamon Press.
Cover design by Adam Craig © Adam Craig from original artwork by Adam Craig.
Cinnamon Press is represented by Inpress.

Praise for *smiling at grief in a house in a forest where life grows:*

In her visually-inventive novel, Jan Fortune not only inhabits the minds of a community of engaging characters who are navigating a fragile future but also proves herself fluent in the language of birch and oak, to be acutely attuned to the song of moss and clover. ...a vital work that grapples with such momentous themes as individual and collective trauma, yet celebrates love, resilience and the intimate, reciprocal relationship between the human and more than human.

Susan Richardson,
author of *Words the Turtle Taught Me* & *Where the Seals Sing*

Deeply rooted and grounded in a loving respect for our living earth and her healing medicines, this heartfelt story weaves magical rhythmic wordspells in a web of vibrant prose. A superb and nurturing work of love, hope and reconnection.

Uma Dinsmore-Tuli,
author of *Yoni Shakti* & *Yoga Nidra Made Easy*

Jan's newest work invites you into an embodied journey through the colors of grief while reconnecting to the natural world. Reading this book is a healing act in its own right.

Yoli Maya Yeh,
Therapist, Educator & Activist

Jan Fortune's new novel is an intriguing exploration of our human connection to the earth and to each other. In a future that feels like the past, a group of forest dwellers grows beyond the trauma of social and environmental collapse, to find wisdom not only through each other but through the plant life that surrounds them. While bleakly prophetic, the novel holds out the possibility of redemption through nature, in human stories interwoven with the subtle scents and secrets of the herbalist's knowledge, lore, and craft. A book to savour for its wide botanical erudition and wise heart.

Catherine Coldstream,
author of *Cloistered: My Years as a Nun*

She pined in thought,
And with a green and yellow melancholy
She sat like patience on a monument,
Smiling at grief. Was not this love indeed?

Twelfth Night, II.iv.111–114

to the forest of La Gare, Berrien & Huelgoat
and for Adam, always

Chapter 1

She'd told Isabelle she would leave at dawn to forage for the last of the ingredients. Still twilight, she whispered to herself, no point lying stiff and unsettled waiting for the light. She pulled on a tattered vest and well-mended shirt, added a sweater the colour of hawthorn leaves darned with swathes of russet wool left over from a jumper that Catherine had knitted years ago. It would ward off the cool before sunrise. She would be in the forest to watch the sun sluicing rivers of colour across the grey-blue morning and keep her own dawn ritual of Alban Hefin. She touched the pendant beneath her clothing and wished Hugo was with her. She had known him for only sixteen months before... No, not today, she whispered, though she knew she was lying to herself. All her ghosts would be with her today. She breathed deeply. Come then, come with me. Help me find the last herbs for the feast. Violets, especially the violets. She

pulled the door to L'Autre Rive closed behind her, stepping
into the day as dawn began to colour the sky to the north-
east of the wood, dusky pinks becoming striations of orange
slowly lifting the white globe of the sun. She stood, drinking
in the glow that softened to yellows as the sun liquified,
pouring itself out. She crossed the track, descending the
steep slope towards the river, breathing in humus and tree
breath. Birch made her think of Isabelle, still asleep before
the long day ahead. She'd gathered buds from the tips of the
branches in Spring, steeped and distilled them with the
small harvest from the Gaultheria shrubs she had seeded in
the forest, extracting powerful wintergreen oil that would
soothe pains. But some of the birch twigs and and buds,
alive with sap, she had kept to make a gentle tree essence,
macerated in a portion of the dwindling supply of brandy, a
remnant from before the Shift, not as old as her beloved
mentor, but almost as potent, smoother and kinder than the
alcohol they made now. Silver essence for a silver woman,

shh   shh   assuaging   soothing   skin to skin   softing-
caressing   shh   shh   decay eating   rot-warding   sorrow
away sorrow   grief bittered to sweet   sweet yielding to tears
cycles and solace   breathe   breathe   coughs spume and ease
etiolate   sap   rage slowing   rapids calming   waters cooling

Lisette had said, savouring the fresh hints of mint and
wintergreen, the cooling astringency beneath the fragrance
of the aged alcohol. The birch trees were in full Summer leaf
now, releasing their clean mintiness into the air after
yesterday's rains and the morning's dew. She would return
soon to collect leaves, fresh for vinegars, dried for teas. But
for now she rested a hand on a papery trunk, bones easing
into the day, muscles relaxing, mind and gut lightening at
the touch. Beneath her feet the birch's fibrous roots fanned
out, shallow and wide. She breathed deeply. Oak on the
breeze, thick and loamy, moss-deep, tang of bitterness
grounding its sweeter notes. Hugo's body laid at the feet of
oaks… She took a fork above the river, stepped between
more roots twining across the surface of the earth, pushed
into the undergrowth. There, the last small clumps of dog
violets, some hanging their delicate heads not yet ready for
the day, others uncurling their heart-shaped petals in the
shade, the shock of their blue-violet veined with indigo

sinew pulsating   shallowing   rooting   searching droplets of
life   moisturing spreading   reaching entwining   drink drink
fibres reaching   rooting   supporting   signalling   talking
fungal threading   one to another   sinew pulsating
drinking in water   soaking up news   shallowing   rooting

threads that met in the creamy white of their centres. She bent down and smoothed a finger over a petal. Viola riviniana, odourless, unlike the the sweet Viola odorata, which was harder to find, though sometimes she came across it—the relics of cultivated gardens... Riviniana would do the same work—clear the lungs, let grief flow out. She would taste as delicate, this Viola riviniana, who would adorn the feast and make a medicine for... Perhaps not, but Isabelle would love the petals. It would be enough. She took a twist of waxed paper from a pouch and unrolled it, dipping her finger into honey and smearing some onto the base of each stand of flowers, asking permission to take some of each plant in return. Carefully, she chose a portion of the heart-shaped leaves and delicate flowers, cutting quickly with her small sharp knife, layering them into another pouch. Each time she touched her hands together in thanks, bowed almost imperceptibly, listened to the plant speak of tears and rivers, waves of grief and lymph, spume of coughs,

assuaging   soothing   soft soft   moving   unfevering
wound balming   eastering   cooling   nourishing
astringing   joying   boundarying   grounding
deflaming   unclotting   unbruising   unwounding
moistening   softing-caress-soothing   sorrow away sorrow

rapids of anger, cooling waters clearing paths with their surge and flow. She nodded and carefully dug up two whole violet plants, lifting the knot of rhizome roots and hairs, tapping the excess earth from their tangles before dropping them into the long, low hessian bag slung across her shoulder. Lost in the slow ritual, she startled when a dog barked sharp high notes into the early daylight. She froze. A series of barks, shorter notes this time. Fragan, she said aloud, calling Deniel to wake. She stood and moved further up the slope, listing other herbs she needed. She brushed her hand over an area of Solomon's seal, remembering the tender shoots they had given in the Spring, the rhizomes she had dried for decoctions and tinctures. For almost two hours she dipped to her knees, leaving a trail of honey smears, cutting with care, thanking and listening. If Fragan barked, if a small mammal moved in the undergrowth, if a voice called her name through the trees, she heard none of it, saturated in the voices of dandelion and nettle, sorrel, ox-

humus   moist dark   sideways reaching   levelling
beneath   decay   feeds   holds   dark-riching
minerals   full-sharp   shade-moisting   nitrogen
crumbling   oxygen pouring   assuaging   moist dark
shade-moisting   dark-riching   assuaging   Shh   shh

13

shh   shh   assuaging   soothing   softing-caressing
rot-warding   sorrow away sorrow   grief bittered to sweet
sweet yielding to tears   cycles and solace   breathe   breathe
coughs and spume ease   etiolate   sap   rage slowing   rapids
calming   waters cooling   bitters healing   loosen   let-go

eye daisy, ground ivy, clover and violet, the plants she passed, and the plants singing in her foraging bag.

Deniel touched her arm lightly. Viola! Fragan was at her thigh, nudging with his shaggy grey head. She shook herself slightly, looked up at Deniel, only a metre in front of her. He smiled, not telling her that she should always stay aware, even after all these years in this place that felt safe and familiar, that she should never let down her guard, they could never know when... But he'd stopped saying it years ago, knowing she would always go into this trance where all she would see and hear were the plants. For a while he'd urged Lisette to go with her. She was so much more vigilant, every sense alert, so different. But it was too much to ask of a child and Viola was her own person. Happy birthday, he said instead. He didn't say he was looking forward to the feast. He still had doubts about the timing of what he had planned for today, but the party would give him the space... and she was forty, not the twenty-three year old who'd

In the earth are words and the words are health
In the earth are words and the words are health
In the earth are words and the words are health
earth   tonify   adapt   replenish   root   soften

in the forest is a world and the world is life
in the forest is a world and the world is life
in the forest is a world and the world is life

repel   boundary   calm   build   warm   light   soak
expand   eat-sun   dry   tighten   sting   balance
attract   protect   flow   uplift   weep   cleanse

travelled from Ireland in the last Autumn before the Shift. And he'd had so much more than most men. She thanked him and he asked her if she had everything she needed for the feast. It was too polite, this exchange, both of them not saying the things they were thinking, as though the momentousness of the day was too much to speak of, the double birthday, the plans he was hiding, the thing she was treating him for, the feast and all the losses stirred by such an occasion. I'm going to sit awhile on my stump, he said and she nodded and smiled, said she would see him later. He watched her go down the slope, watched Fragan consider going with her before the two of them turned towards the river and the stump that was his favourite resting place. He'd sat here after they'd buried Hugo fifteen years ago. He'd be sixty-two if he'd lived, ten years his junior, twenty years his step-son's senior. Alex was another miracle of survival like himself. Alex had been sick with something undiagnosable for the two years before the Bane came, taking old and

ancestor-deeping   tapping tapping   rooting down tapping
lateralling widing   remembering crown   storing the story
memorying branches long days keeping   wisdoming peacing
knowledging cooling   unpoisoning   unbleeding   holding
unwounding   release tonic cleanse   ancestor-deeping

15

young, frail and healthy, but always more men than women. Like a war from history. But unlike those long ago battlegrounds, the casualties were not concentrated in a generation. And yet... two men surviving in one household, but they'd lost Beth in the first month. It had been too much for her, staying alive, not knowing what had happened to the daughter she saw only every three or four years, half way round the planet when all communication had ceased, and having nightmares about her twin daughters in England, a place that had not seemed distant but suddenly might as well have been on another planet. He'd sensed she wanted it to take her, but it had taken him a long time to forgive her for succumbing to it so easily. Viola had come to study with her. And with Isabelle and Hugo. They had been a powerful team. Still were, even after Beth... even after Hugo... He'd always felt himself lesser. Not in a resentful way, simply that he didn't have their clarity, that surety of vocation. After the Bane came the Shift and his talents felt even more uncertain, though his music was welcome and, for a man who had never felt skilled in practical things, he and Alex both learnt quickly, despite the frustrations of there being no Internet videos to watch and copy. He sighed and Fragan looked up from nosing through leaf mulch and whined softly. You'll be okay, old boy, he said to the dog, who shook himself and came close, nudging his hand so that he scratched the hound's head. You'll be okay. Fragan laid down at his feet and he thought again about this stump, how the living trees kept stumps alive, sent them sugars through the mycelia to preserve the elder's knowledge even after death. Humans did it differently, passing on ideas and stories. Come on, old boy. Lot to do today, we'd better be going. Fragan lumbered to his feet and trotted alongside him, not towards their low L-shaped longère, its roof slightly sagging but propped inside and still keeping out the elements, but towards L'Autre Rive, its familiar square three storeys surrounded by herb and vegetable beds, its verge cheerful with ox-eye

protecting   salving   immuning   adapting
hepatic   strengthening   digesting   defending
infection-dispelling   unfevering   unflaming
unpaining   contracting   dissolving   welling
unsoring   emetic   flowing   analgesing   toning

daisies tracking the sun, the spit set up on what had once been a small car park at the front, long tables down the near side of the building and carboys of cider that would be placed at the far end of the tables later in the day. Behind the house, a long polytunnel had been preserved through the years. They still had bails of plastic unused, but eventually… Inside, its beds contained the herbs hardest to grow in the Breton climate, even in these warmer times—astragalus, codonopsis and turmeric amongst them, allies that Viola had prescribed for him over the last year, no, longer than that… She had seeded berberis and goldenseal amongst the trees, cultivated bloodroots to transplant into the forest, where butcher's broom already grew wild. Cat's claw was kept in pots, vines of it dotted around houses in the hamlet, pruned and controlled. Every house in the settlement had beds of herbs—sheep's sorrel in the sunniest gardens, milk thistle in their borders, echinacea in the well-drained beds that enjoyed periods of shade as well as sun, lawns of

unplaquing   cooling   anxious no more   nourishing
time to digest   bittering   soothing   cough will be gone
upbuilding   supporting   breathe easy again   unsugaring
unbruising   lean on this strength   lymphing   unulcering
energy here   unbloating   balancing   let the heart rest

feverfew and others of chamomile, the artemesias—mugwort, wormwood and sweet Annie—in the dryer soils along the fringes of the old roads. These and others, grown and foraged to supply her pharmacy that served not only the dozen inhabited buildings between Kerkoad and the Gite d'Artus, but also those who came from the small communities left in Berrien and La Gare. In Huelgoat and Poullaouen, Isabelle and Viola had trained others to plant and forage, to make decoctions and tinctures for their neighbours, though sometimes they would still arrive for advice, lacking Viola's confidence with the more powerful plants like mistletoe, his mainstay since she'd began treating him. He stopped under the shade of the trees at the bend before the house. He'd taken the longer route back with its gentler slope and paused to watch Alex, who was already at the spit, the boar beginning to heat for the long ten hours it would take. It was only moments before Alex looked up and waved, Fragan bounding forward happily. Looks like you've

in the forest is a world and the world is life
in the forest is a world and the world is life
in the forest is a world and the world is life

made a good start already, Deniel said, approaching the roast. Alex nodded. I was up here before seven. Viola got back about twenty minutes ago. Going to be a hot day.

He looks tired before the day's hardly started, Alex thought, giving the carcass a turn. More yellow in his eyes today, but at least he's been for a walk. Go far? he asked. Deniel shook his head. Just to the old stump—my thinking spot. Alex pursed his lips, but said nothing. So not a real walk. I'm going indoors for chopping duty, Deniel added, but I can come out and spell you in a bit. Gaëlle-Anne should be here soon, but I'll shout if we need any help. He wondered if his voice sounded too cheery, too forced, but Deniel smiled and nodded. He watched his step-father carefully. Were his steps more halting or was he over-thinking this? He'd be glad when Gaëlle-Anne arrived. She had a way of being optimistic without the sense that she was simply saying what others wanted to hear. She simply saw the best, something he found difficult. Something he'd

in the earth are words and the words are health
in the earth are words and the words are health
in the earth are words and the words are health

in the forest is a world and the world is life
in the forest is a world and the world is life
in the forest is a world and the world is life

always had in common with Deniel, making the first years after his mother died hard on both of them. But they had found a rhythm in learning skills together and it had helped when Gaëlle-Anne moved in with them. Ten years they'd been a couple. He'd never imagined himself a father, even in the days when the world seemed a more certain place. He laughed at himself. He'd never thought of the world as a place of security, though his pessimism hadn't helped him predict the details of the Shift or the enormity of everyone's losses. Yet here he was, roasting a boar that he had helped catch, preparing a birthday feast for people he cared about, waiting for his partner to arrive with their children. Fragan came out of the house and settled close to him, his nose dancing to the scent of the cooking meat. It'll be a while yet, boy. Fragan sighed and laid his large shaggy head on long paws. Patience on a monument, eh? he quipped to the dog. He turned the spit again and heard his children before he caught sight of them. Twin boys. Was the world righting

in the earth are words and the words are health
in the earth are words and the words are health
in the earth are words and the words are health

in the forest is a world and the world is life
in the forest is a world and the world is life
in the forest is a world and the world is life

itself slowly? He remembered the morning of their birth, Gaëlle-Anne joking about being the only woman she'd ever heard of living in a house of four men. What had she done to deserve this? He'd marvelled that she could find humour after the hours of labour, but she'd had good care, Viola administering teas and diffusing the oils she made in her still, Carène calm and encouraging, happy to be using her skills as a midwife. They would be eight in September. How had that happened? They ran towards him, speaking at once, and he was overcome with a moment of utter sadness, an image of his nephew one Christmas, aged about eight, visiting from England with his parents, full of life... What had happened to him? What had become of his sisters— three of them disappeared into a world without phones, without post... He shook himself and held out his arms as Ronan and Paol ran towards him, Gaëlle-Anne smiling behind them.

in the earth are words and the words are health
in the earth are words and the words are health
in the earth are words and the words are health

in the forest is a world and the world is life, above, below, root and branch, leaf and root, root and flower, as above, the flower nursing aeons, this atom of leaf that was atom of mollusc, this sliver of bark once cells of the hart's

Chapter 2

Viola watched Deniel chopping. She'd insisted he sit at the long table, beyond what had once been a café bar, to work. He was quiet and looked older by the day, his skin grey. But it was the yellowing in his eyes that concerned her more and she was sure there was also some bloating. She wanted to ask him how the back pain was, whether the constipation was worse or his appetite even less, but this was a chopping party, not a consultation. In any case, she could see the signs—it had spread from bowel to liver and now she suspected there were ascites. Could she drain the fluid? It would give some relief from the pressure, but what of the pain of the incision? Would a strong tincture of clove, thyme and datura be sufficient? She would talk to Isabelle, but didn't want to tire her, not today on their shared birthday. How many ninety-three year olds might there be in the world now? Isabelle was thirteen years Claire's senior, sixteen

in the forest is a world and the world is life, above, below, root and branch, leaf and root, root and flower, as above, the flower nursing aeons, this atom of leaf that was atom of mollusc, this sliver of bark once cells of the hart's *beating* heart. *a leaf of grass is no less than the journey work of the stars.* listen. once upon all time, always upon every time, in the forest is a world and the world is life, and the forest is one and the world is one, and all is life

years older than Élodie and could give Deniel twenty-one years, the oldest of their small group of elders by far, but there she was in the kitchen, chopping and stirring, bustling around with Lisette as they worked together. If only Hugo were here. Fifteen years and she would never get used to his absence.

She walked through the long terminal building past the information desk and grey plastic chairs, the shiny black floor slightly squeaking with the weight of her pack, laden with everything she might need for a two-year stay. A line of cars stood outside the glass doors marked 'arrivée' and she scanned the people standing beside them. There, the man in the plum sweater, waving and walking towards her, undoubtedly the person Oisín had painted as the Hierophant in his tarot deck—teacher, mentor, wise ancestor, interpreter of sacred mysteries. Her grandfather had painted him not as an aged priest but a youth seated in

and the forest is one and the world is one, and all is life every time, in the forest is a world and the world is life, work of the stars. listen. once upon all time, always upon beating heart. a leaf of grass is no less than the journey and death, death a passage through life, as above, so below, decay to life, rotting to recycle, dissolution to rebuild, worm becoming toe of dog becoming fingernail of musician becoming petal of rose becoming root of oak

a lotus position beneath a large hazel tree, holding a key that ended in a pentangle. When Oisín did the painting Hugo would have been a baby, not the young man he'd foreseen. The man standing in front of her was in his early 40s, remarkably unchanged either from her grandfather's picture or the person she had met briefly at her grandmother's funeral eight years ago—light brown hair curling in knots, intelligent hazel eyes. In the picture he'd worn a blue tunic over fawn yoga trousers, a stag watching from the background. Welcome to the end of the world, Viola Róisin Jacobs Ó Murcháin MacAonghusa, he said to her, smiling. She grinned. Finistère. Yes, a name bequeathed by the Romans, but in Breton, Penn-ar-Bed, both the end and start of the world. Most endings are also beginnings, she agreed, a sudden tongue of wind curling around her so that she shivered for a moment. Can I take your pack? he offered. I'm fine. Which is your car? He led the way down the row of waiting cars to a small black Peugeot and lifted the lid of

musician becoming petal of rose becoming root of oak rebuild, worm becoming toe of dog becoming fingernail of below, decay to life, rotting to recycle, dissolution to and death, death a passage through life, as above, so becoming… a different story, this sapling oak containing *gneiss, coal, long-threaded moss, fruits, grains, esculent roots,* this moth that was shitake's body, *and mossy scabs of the worm fence, heap'd stones, elder, mullein* and *poke-*

the boot for her to slide the pack into. Isabelle is so excited to meet you again, he said, as he pulled the car out onto the road. And me her. I wasn't in a very good space to talk to her at Sarah's funeral and then I felt I'd missed an opportunity. We have the same birthday and she knew my grandparents when they lived near Paimpont. She and Sarah used to email constantly. How did you come to know her? She watched him carefully, long fingers on the steering wheel, a way of taking his time that made her feel restful. A friend of your mother's, the daughter of your mother's sister's best friend to be precise… Miriam, she asked? Yes, Miriam. She met Isabelle in Toledo when she was studying for her MA. Isabelle was living in Spain and used to visit the museum where Miriam worked. As you know, Isabelle had been staying with your grandparents, with Sarah and Oisín, the Summer he died and Oisín had given her one of this tarot sets that they'd had printed. There were only five or six sets, she interjected. My grandmother had the originals. They

of the worm fence, heap'd stones, elder, mullein and poke- roots, this moth that was shitake's body, and mossy scabs gneiss, coal, long-threaded moss, fruits, grains, esculent becoming… a different story, this sapling oak containing

weed are the world, are the universe, are the forest and
the forest is a world and the world is life. linger. the world
is here, under and over, as above so… the oak asks, *what
is the grass?* flesh of earth's flesh, flesh of oak's flesh, flesh

passed to my mother with two sets of the copies. No one
seems to know what happened to the others, apart from the
ones Oisín gave to Isabelle. How strange that they went to
Miriam. Her partner was a distant relative of ours. He
nodded. Casilda? Yes. My grandmother was French and her
sister married a Hungarian artist. Casilda was her great-
granddaughter, I think, and Miriam's family had been
connected to ours in odd ways for generations. Tangled
stories, Hugo said, like the tale of Oisín's Brocéliande Tarot.
Isabelle gave the cards to Miriam who gave them to me,
loaned them initially. You read my mother's tarot with them
when she visited you in Prague? When she, she was… Hugo
nodded slowly. When she was a ghost, yes. Just before your
father rescued her from the Otherworld. She felt the cold
breath of wind again, though the car windows and air vents
were closed. Do you still have them? she asked. Yes. Me and
Isabelle use them still. They've seen a lot of wear, but we take
good care of them. She shot him a puzzled glance. Did

weed are the world, are the universe, are the forest
and the forest is a world and the world is life. linger. the oak
world is here, under and over, as above, so… the oak
asks, what is the grass? flesh of earth's flesh, flesh of oak's

Miriam and Isabelle stay in touch? I mean, if it was Miriam who gave you the cards how did you get to meet Isabelle? He smiled. No, I think Isabelle appeared in Miriam's life and disappeared soon after. She was moving back to Paris after being in Toledo. Like you, I met her for the first time at your grandmother's funeral. I didn't know Sarah, but your mother asked me to be there. I'd always stayed in touch with Saoirse. When we went back to Reagh after the ceremony Isabelle walked up to me and said, So you're Oisín's hierophant. Hugo, isn't it? I think Miriam passed the cards to you. And, to make it more weird, it felt completely normal, like I'd known her all my life. Do you have a set of your dad's tarot with you? Yes—one of the copies and Saoirse insisted I bring the originals too. Hugo took his eyes off the road for the first time since their journey had begun. Was that anxiety? His calm and focus were back in place in a moment, but a wave of nausea rose in her gullet. It disturbs you that Saoirse gave me the originals? He pursed

of all flesh, it is grass that was a different story, that died, was reborn, will be another story and... the beautiful uncut hair of graves come to life to die again, and to die is different from what any one supposed, and luckier.

his lips, taking his time. I'm not sure I'd say it disturbs me, but it's a big gesture. They were probably the most personal thing she had of her father's. She nodded, remembering Saoirse's resolution when she'd said she didn't want to risk travelling with the cards, that she'd be home in two years and the time would go in a blink. Is my mother sick do you think? She felt queasy forming the words, but his reply was immediate. No. I'd know if she were. She's well. He smiled. She'll have a good reason. And your father? How is Faolán? Also well, she confirmed. They continued in silence for a while, but as they drew closer, the car winding through roads with forest on either side, he began to tell her about the places and people close to home. You also first met Isabelle in Ireland I think? She nodded. Yes, but we didn't speak much. I was too… He nodded in turn. Isabelle's what? she asked, seventy-six now? She is. Hugo chuckled. Don't tell her that though. No, no one would guess, she thought, as the car pulled into the gravelled space in front of L'Autre

mountain beside a river where salmon might swim and
hedge of hawthorn and yew twist and turn, turn and twist,
dead-ending, mischieving, gathering round the hazel of
knowledge where the ground is prickly with yew and

Rive and a woman rose from a garden table to greet them—
it was eight years since her grandmother's funeral but
Isabelle seemed unchanged—slender and elegant with pale
golden hair, beautiful, like spun silk, and, as she approached
with outstretched arms, even paler blue eyes.

She came back to the kitchen, the same pale blue eyes
looking at her with concern. You were a long way away,
Isabelle said. I was thinking about Hugo. And my parents
too. Isabelle put a hand on her arm. She's still at Reagh,
Isabelle said quietly. But not Faolán, she replied, wishing she
hadn't added this to Isabelle's attempt at reassurance. She'd
known from the outset that the Bane took so many more
men than women, but she'd clung to the thought that her
father was strong, it wouldn't take Faolán, she'd told herself
constantly, until the day Hugo looked at her with more
sorrow than she could bear to see. Hugo had always had a
link to Saoirse, even before the Internet vanished and letters

the hazel of knowledge where the ground is prickly with
and twist, dead-ending, mischieving, gathering round
turn, turn and yew twist and turn, turn and twist, turn
mountain beside a river where salmon might swim and hedge

thorns and once upon Saoirse's time their low green voice scratched ears as thorns scratch skin and the hazel asked for a memory and sighed sharp green, maze of hawthorn, hazel, yew where Oisín was raised, listening to voices of

stopped. He'd always known whether her mother was well or ill, content or sad. When she'd asked him about it, he'd wave his hands either side of his head, laughing—Maybe it's because I'm 'different', maybe because the first time I met your mother she was a ghost and I'd just lost my parents. We met in a state of extremity. Sometimes she'd envied him his bond with Saoirse, but when the Shift came and he could tell her that Saoirse and Faolán were safe, she was relieved, until that day… And then it was…

He put down the cards and sat so still she began to feel uneasy. Hugo? He shook himself slightly and smiled—a thin, sad smile. Let's do the reading another day, he said. There's something I want to teach you. Or… teach probably isn't the right word. He made the gesture of rubbing his hands either side of his ears without touching them, the signal for what he called his 'difference'. Something I'd like to… like you to be able to do. She waited for him to go on.

of hawthorn, hazel, yew where Oisín was raised, listening to hazel asked for a memory and sighed sharp green, maze green voice scratched ears as thorns scratch skin and the low their time Saoirse's upon once and thorns leaf and branch, root and seed, that were voices of wind, songs of light, where Faolán met Saoirse, where Sarah scattered Saoirse's ashes years before Saoirse scattered Sarah's ashes as Viola wept beside the hazel that

So you can keep in touch with Saoirse, for yourself. How? she asked, other questions falling silent between them. Why now? What...? I'm fine, Hugo said, but these are challenging times. It would be good if we could both know she's well. Isabelle knows how she is, doesn't she? she'd asked. Yes, he'd said. There are others she senses too—people from her past, but it would be good for you too. She'd nodded, steadying her breathing...

Birthdays are strange times, aren't they? Isabelle's question brought her back to the present again. She blinked. Yes. I always feel guilty about having so many memories and yearnings, but I can never stop them flooding back. Deniel chipped in from beyond the bar. I feel the same, I think of Beth every day, but birthdays and feast days... it's always more poignant somehow. The bittersweet, Isabelle said softly. Try some of the sweet, Lisette put in, holding out a spoon for her mother to taste. Wonderful! You used some of

Saoirse scattered Sarah's ashes as Viola wept beside the where Sarah scattered Saoirse's ashes years before voices of wind, songs of light, where Faolán met Saoirse, to voices of leaf and branch, root and seed, that were

mourned in light and sang a green lament and yew
whispered the long view of becoming ancestor, death
ceding to life and hawthorn hummed of heart and yew,
hazel whispered seeds of a forest, an ocean and a country

the fruit from the pygmy date palms? Lisette nodded. I'm
going to make a custard later and pears baked in honey. We
won't want to eat for a week after this, she said, smiling at
her daughter. Speak for yourself. I'm going to gorge on
leftovers for as long as they last. Such poise and confidence,
she thought, as Lisette pulled Isabelle back to their tasks at
the kitchen counter. Deniel stood and carried a large tray of
chopped veg to the bar. Ready for my next assignment, he
said. Yours to command. Hmm—too early to chop the
salads. Consider it an official rest period. Deniel nodded,
but said, I'll go and see how Alex is getting on. She thought
of calling after him that he should take some rest while there
was time but stopped herself. Don't fuss. He knows when he
needs to listen to his body. She watched him bend to chat
with Ronan and Paol, the boys gesturing and animated as
they talked. She watched Alex surreptitiously eyeing his
step-father, no doubt asking himself the same questions that
were in her mind. She felt Lisette lean against her and put

hawthorn, hazel whispered seeds of a forest, an ocean and
ceding to life and hawthorn hummed of heart and yew,
yew whispered the long view of successor becoming, death
hazel that mourned in light and sang a green lament and

her arms around her waist. He'll be fine, Lisette said, as Deniel set off in the direction of his longère. See, he's going for a break without you even ordering him to. Did you get everything you wanted from the forest? She turned towards her daughter, still standing in the ring of her arms. I did. Shall I make us some tea before I get into cooking? Fantastic idea, Isabelle called. Make a couple of big pots. Reinforcements should be here soon.

Deniel walked slowly, Fragan loping alongside. Can't stand waiting beside all those cooking scents, eh, old boy? Well, let's see what we have for you at home. In the cool of the kitchen he stood looking at the row of powders and tinctures that had become his routine over the last seventeen months. He remembered asking Viola about using yew, some study he'd heard of years ago but she was adamant that it was too dangerous. It's not like we can get pharmaceutical extracts any more, she'd warned. She'd told him there was no antidote. Even in hospitals all they could do was give

healing unworded, that grows in tree and herb, in mushroom and shrub, in berry and bud, healing-pulsing light and death, dark and life, healing sweet as yew's scarlet aril, bitter as adieu. linger. in the forest is a world

activated charcoal, try to control the arrythmias, support the person with electrolytes and resuscitate if necessary. She'd also discounted amygdalin from the seeds of bitter almonds, plums, cherries and other fruits. My books don't have enough information, she'd told him, and as far as I remember, all the evidence of its effects on cancer were studies in vitro. And even then I have a feeling that it mostly limited proliferation in bladder and breast cancers. He'd always appreciated her honesty, knowing that at best she was giving him a little more time. Time—unlike Beth, he'd seen Alex flourish into a skilled member of the community, a loving partner and good father. He'd had years of Gaëlle-Anne's warmth and humour, been part of his grandchildren's lives. Though he ached for Beth every day on waking, the list of blessings would always outrun any litany of if-onlies… His grief had been a bond with Viola when she'd lost Hugo only six months after Beth had gone. He was glad that he and Beth had played their part in the

scarlet aril, bitter as adieu. linger. in the forest is a world light and death, dark and life, healing sweet as yew's mushroom and shrub, in berry and bud, healing-pulsing that is healing unworded, that grows in tree and help, in

and the world is life and it calls… listen, linger, here is
all that is green, all that is needful, all that has been and
will ever be, here is the universe in ripening bramble,
creation in the dew on a lady's mantle leaf, here is food,

flourishing of that relationship.

But it's not just a matter of six years like you and Deniel, Hugo was saying to Beth when he walked into the kitchen of their longère, the low Winter sun pooling on the pale scrubbed oak table. Tell him it's fine, Beth said with mock exasperation. What's fine? He'd looked from Beth to Hugo. You're kidding me! Everyone and their dog can see he's besotted. Everyone but you and Viola apparently. He grinned. Yeah, you're right. Annick was just saying yesterday she could see it coming a mile off. He patted the head of the shaggy blue-grey dog at his side. Hugo laughed, his strained expression dissolving for a moment before his face clouded again. But you said you don't think Viola realises? She might be appalled. She… I'm twenty-two years older. It's… He threw up his hands. Annick made her whine of bored yawning and flopped onto the floor, head on her paws. See. He grinned, pulling out a chair and sitting next to Hugo.

fruit, creation in the dew on a lady's mantle leaf, here is
will ever be, here is the universe in ripening bramble,
all that is green, all that is needful, all that has been and
and the world is life and it calls… listen, linger, here is

song, medicine, poison, here is story of all that can be, wound in an acorn, patterned in mugwort, papered in birch bark, dappling in light, in the forest is a world and the world is life. listen. linger. connect. it is enough.

Annick says you'd be a fool not to go for it. He held up a hand as Hugo began to object again. Look Hugo, the world's a weird place. We might be a bit insulated from the political insanity and tantrums of late capitalism here in the sticks, but we still know things aren't good out there. As far as everyone else can see, you and Viola just belong together. Why don't you let her decide if the age difference is a problem? Beth nodded emphatically. Cake anyone?

He felt Fragan's snout nosing into his hand as he rested against the kitchen counter. I promised you a snack, didn't I, boy? My mind wandered away a bit there—I was remembering your great-grandmother—looked just like you, old Annick—bit shorter, I guess, but exactly your coat and eyes. Fragan waited patiently for him to walk to the fridge and begin filling an old dish with offal. I'll get you some fresh water with that, eh? He'd rest now. Rest then write what was needed before returning to the feast.

song of all that can ever be, wound in an acorn, patterned in a mugwort leaf, papered into birch bark, dappling in the dancing light, in the forest is a world and the world is life.

Chapter 3

She watched the steady influx of neighbours carrying pots and trays, baskets and crates into the garden or to the door of L'Autre Rive, admiring how they slipped into roles, as though none of them ever snapped at one another or screamed into the forest that they would never talk to this one or that one again... Thirty-two adults and eleven children, though Zoé, already fifteen, and Lisette a few months shy of fifteen, would no doubt object to being lumped into this category. At the far side of the garden, Sébastien, Zélie and Francine were forming a team erecting gazebos and awnings. They were joined by Gilles, while his partner, Véronique, their daughter, Zoé, and her brother, Pierrick, gathered children from the arriving families, some to be entertained, others to be given tasks to make them feel essential to operations. Élodie, Veronique's mother, tiny but spritely at seventy-seven, began to separate the younger

deer, human and fox, welcome to the company, we hear in our gut, our heart, our bones, come forest together for the forest is a world and the world is life. listen, the company calls—come Isabelle, Hugo, come Alex, come Émilie,

children to follow her to the gather-hall, where her son, Alain, and his partner, Hervé, would take turns storytelling and organising impromptu puppet shows between spells hefting crates and barrels. Five-year-old Pascal darted from the side of his heavily pregnant mum, Julie, to join his friend, Armel, while Armel's older sister, Gigi, scanned the forming groups, uncertain whether a ten-year-old should be going with the little ones. She watched her dither, saved when her friend Joceline, a year older, Sébastien and Zélie's youngest, sidled up, announcing loudly that she and Gigi wouldn't mind helping with 'the kids'. Ronan and Paol joined the troupe, leaving André shuffling from foot to foot. Help me get this lot into the hall, Pierrick called over to him. Then we can go help bring crates from the houses. She watched André grin his relief and Zoé clap her brother's back affectionately. Great, she said, me and Alice can go help Lisette. Alice looked up, standing hunched near a gazebo still waiting for its covering, so much less sure of

of thunder, the sounds you cannot hear; we must wind through the earth, folding on ourselves, rich and dense. listen, it is enough to come into the forest for the forest is a world and the world is life, all of life forest and as below

herself than her sister, Joceline, despite being three years older. So the children have organised themselves, she thought. And the adults? Today, barring the odd barb that might slip out after too much cider or exhaustion, they would all be determined to make everything go well. She knew it was a gesture of goodwill towards her—those who loved her and those who found her distant, too closed and hard to read, were united in thanking the stars that they had a skilled herbalist in running distance of their homes. But even more, they wanted to celebrate Isabelle. Ninety-three! Isabelle had exclaimed the evening before. It's a ridiculous number. Nothing special about it at all. But each year they all wondered if the next number would be reached, despite Isabelle's sharp mind and indomitable elegance. And, quite apart from the double birthdays, it was Summer Solstice, everyone's festival, everyone's day when memories would surface, many good, more unbearable. And yet they did bear them—Aimée, who'd made a good life with Carène and had

hawthorn, hazel of wisdom, whispering journey. to
Huelgoat, to wild rose, to birch, ash and oak. listen.
company calling to eldering forest, magnetic as
lodestone, attractive as cobalt, gathering our own year

her two grown daughters, Anna and Joëlle, close by, but still
mourned her husband, who had been one of the earliest to
die. Marie-Claude, who had lost husband and sons, but
whose daughter, Cloé, lived in the house of four noisy
twenty-something young women who hunted and fished
and had grown up tough and skilful. Anna, Joëlle, Cloé and
Cynthia had been seven to ten when the world changed and
if they remembered much from their early years they kept it
to themselves. Cynthia's mother, Brigitte, made a home with
her sister, Diane, each keeping their losses close, but
thankful that they had their mother, Claire, who was eighty,
the second oldest in the community. Claire had buried her
farming husband and two sons but one son survived,
together with her girls, Christophe was now the community
potter and his partner, Enora, was skilled at weaving, dyeing
and reviving any remnant of fabric, between raising André,
Gigi and Armel. She waved to Julie to come inside—six
months pregnant and looking well, but hot, Noé at her side,

bounty, rippling our joy. we are labyrinth and nest. we are
here for all. we are the pathways that connect all life. we
are the underground tongues of the trees. listen. in the
earth are words and the words are health, the words are

upon year, oaks dropping acorns that germinate saplings, mother trees choosing those that will thrive, goats birthing kids, bees swarming new hives, blackthorn seeding, swallows nesting, humans homing, a single

earnest and solicitous. The rest of the beekeepers were arriving, Marie-Claude's sister, Ghislaine, another who'd lost her husband, but her daughters Nicole and Caroline were with her, bearing the sweetness of the bees with them. Only Catherine and Émilie had not yet arrived. They had walked into the hamlet one day after the Bane had subsided and the Shift had changed everything, gaunt and dazed, with stories they still had not told after sixteen years. They lived in a small stone house between the two longères, helped Sébastien, Zélie and Francine with the crops and the noisy girls with preserving their catches. Somewhere in their late fifties or early sixties, she guessed, both well-read, unassuming and rarely asking her for help from the herbs. She walked behind L'Autre Rive to scan the road. There they were. Did they confide in each other, she wondered. Even their walk was stiff. How many years can a person hold in unspoken trauma and go on seeming to function… no, not seeming—they contributed as much as anyone, and yet…

grow to the growl of thunder, to the throb of vibration that sings through our filaments, strings of the forest's music. we grow and we give, sensing the sound waves, mycelia sings a world of nourishment into the roots, sharing our forest, each for itself, each for all, separate species, a single company, one forest where nettle is boundary, nettle builds blood, leaves of blackcurrant catch sunlight for food, protect from insects, ward disease, sage aromatic

But this was not the day for such thoughts. She smiled and waved and they saluted in turn. At last they were gathered at L'Autre Rive, all but Deniel, though she was glad he was resting. Now she could host the feast. She returned to the other side of the building, banged the old gong that hung outside the heavy black metal door and called into the moment of silence—Tea's ready. Some to take to the hall, the rest I'll bring out here. What are we having? Alex called back. Zestea. We need the energy and focus, but I'll make something digestive later before we overeat! She savoured the laughter, chose nettle, blackcurrant leaf, sage, rosemary, dandelion leaf and root and a touch of eleuthero. A tea for every occasion. Zestea was a favourite with most, but inside she would make a fresh batch of Isabelle's beloved Breathitea, a blend of lime flowers, self heal, olive leaf, couch grass and rose petals, a small birthday gift to nurture her mentor and friend.

Isabelle sipped the tea. Wonderful. I feel so looked after

filaments of connection, rhythm waving into words that are story of forest that is world, that is all, that knows no separation, that listens, that relates, we grow to the sound of rumbling, sound of pressure falling though humus, we

43

with thujone, repelling invaders; feeding, cleansing,
warm rosemary remembers, soothes and de-stresses,
barring mosquitos, dandelion grounds, nourishing with
root, flowing with leaf, eleuthero for energy, lime to soothe

when you make this, she said. She sat at a small table
cupping the tea bowl in her hands, white porcelain with
flecks of brighter white caught in its surface. She had bought
it many years ago when she was living in the Latin Quarter,
one of a set, the sole survivor now. What had made her pack
it when her old friends had persuaded her to move to the
forest all those years ago? Béatrice and Michel had been
telling her for years that she should move out of the city. On
every visit they'd tell her about interesting houses she might
buy, but when had they become more insistent? Had they
predicted the Shift or was it just obvious to anyone with eyes
and ears open that when the cracks began to widen the cities
would become places of savagery? It had been the visit after
Sarah died when she realised how concerned they really
were. Was that 2040? Sarah had outlived her husband by
thirty-six years. She had lost a sister young too and almost
lost her daughter. Saoirse and Faolán were in their mid-
forties when she'd travelled to Ireland for the funeral. She'd

are the unselfed for all life is network, we are belonging,
which all must inhabit to thrive on this earth, we are
relationship, a word for forest and in the underland of
forest is the story and the story is unwording into

44

membranes, quiet the heart, bring ladybirds home, self heal for butterflies, self heal for throats, for bees, inflammation, self heal for gut, olive pulsating with sun, circulation, easing, unflaming, couch grass to soften,

kept in touch with Sarah since that day in Brocéliande when Oisín's heart had stopped, leaving Saoirse without a father at the age of nine, but neither had travelled to the other's country since then, despite constantly emailing that perhaps next year… Viola had been fifteen, heart-broken at the loss of her grandmother and wanting to be alone as much as possible. She'd travelled back from Ireland by ferry and Michel and Béatrice had met her at Roscoff and driven her to their house in the hamlet near Berrien. There's an amazing place for sale, Béatrice had told her almost as soon as she was settled in the car. It used to be a bookshop and vegan café. Wonderful place—not something you'd expect miles from nowhere in the middle of a forest but always popular—really good books—radical politics and herbalism, proper literature and translations, excellent children's section. I'm sixty-eight, Béa. You think I'm going to run a radical bookshop and café? It would be a great base for your herbs, Michel had put in. Ghislaine and Rémy had

invisible threads, spin stories of what lies beneath, we bring the offerings, we tremble in prayer, we are the treaties, we are the tenders of all that is needful under the ground, we are the messengers of conflict and peace, we cleanse, clear blockage, lacewings and bees gather round roses, nervine, lymphatic rose of the heart, astringe what needs binding, sweet after grief. so many substances, life bloods of plants, essence of trees, calling to insects,

decided it would be a good place for their honey and candle-making too. They had energy, those two, a huge vegetable garden, bees and two young daughters—Nicole four and Caroline six. But Isabelle had never run a café or a shop. She was retired and… And yet she had gone to see it. She'd gone because she had met Hugo at Sarah's funeral. She had been aware of him for a long time and had known when she left the cards with Miriam that they would find their way to Oisín's unusually young and unhierarchical hierophant, and that one day their paths would cross. She'd wandered around L'Autre Rive enchanted with the place. At dinner that night Ghislaine and Rémy joined them, even more excited than Béa and Michel. She'd tried not to give them too much encouragement. Really, they could do this without her, find someone more local as a partner… But she'd told them there was someone she had to speak to, perhaps if he was interested… There were jokes about her secret lover. Strange, she felt forcefully connected to Hugo,

conscious, we sing songs of warning, carry food through choosing, memory-making, mycelia flex, resourceful, unconsciousness, mycelia connect and adapt, sensitive, that's ceased to exist, that never created, ungenerative,

mammals and birds, signalling reptiles, whispering to
humans in voices of light, so many stories weaving a
forest, gathering a company, singing of home. listening
they came. From Morlaix and Paris, Roscommon and

but he'd never be that, not even if she were thirty years
younger or he thirty years older. She'd invited him to Paris
at the funeral, but when she returned from Brittany he'd
persuaded her that they should meet in Prague. It's a city of
alchemy he told her and I think it might be the last chance
either of us will get to spend time there. His other reason for
the choice of Prague he told her only when she arrived—
Miriam and her wife, Casilda, were there. It had been good
to be together in that place. They'd kept in touch afterwards.
They still did. There were those she could sense long after
conventional forms of communication disappeared. It
wasn't the same as long emails and video calls, but at least
she knew they were alive and surviving. She tipped the small
teapot that Viola had filled for her to find it empty. Think
you drained that one, Lisette said, leaning over the counter.
Lisette looked exactly like her grandmother and great-
grandmother—Sarah, Saoirse, Lisette… but Viola followed
a different model, favouring Faolán—thick russet hair and

yes, we're conscious of ridges, of space, of constriction,
encounters en route, remembering, learning, changing
our patterns of growth, mycelia once were known as the
wood wide web, but we're so much more than the network

Prague, they followed the voices of plants to a forest that is world, a world that is life, and as the world changed with its fires and floods, and while the earth echoed with human grief, the forest persisted, living, continually

fair skin that coloured easily. They were different in character too—Lisette had Hugo's calm, his sense of surety without arrogance, a way of seeming older and wiser than her age. Do you want another pot?, Lisette asked. She shook her head. I should be getting back to work. Me, Zoé and Alice have you covered and it's your birthday. Don't you dare tell me to rest, she shot back, but she was laughing as she spoke and perhaps she would go upstairs with a book for half an hour. From her room on the third floor she looked down on her bustling friends and neighbours. Noé had taken over the boar roast from Alex, while the noisy girls spatchcocked chickens over another fire. André, Pierrick and Joceline were lining one end of a long table with plates and cutlery, directed by Enora, Christophe and Aimée hefting a crate of glasses to the other end. Everywhere was activity. Even Catherine and Émilie were mingling, helping Sébastien and Marie-Claude to set a small candle in the centre of every table. She sighed. Viola should blend those

throughout the whole earth, impulse and pulse, electric and flow, nerve signalling nerve, feeling it all, each hypha exquisite with sensing, yes, we aware of all that surrounds, of molecules entering each cell, of ions in flow.

offering shelter and food, nectar for bees, mulch for insects, each kind of medicine for each kind of life, pulsing messages, nourishment through the mycelia, across the forest and far beyond, miles beyond, hundreds

two a talking tea, she said aloud to no-one. But maybe they were right to keep their secrets close.

Émilie looked up. Was she being watched? It was Isabelle, smiling at all of them. She smiled back and waved, but Isabelle had already turned into her room. Happy birthday, she whispered, setting down the last of the candles. Viola had brought out more tea and she thought she'd go and get another cup. The heat of the day was building and the tea refreshing. She'd like to walk with her cup to somewhere quiet, already feeling overwhelmed. These people had been kind to her and Catherine since they'd arrived. Not that she always liked all of them. She found Anna, Joëlle, Cloé and Cynthia rough and loud. She reminded herself they were also skilful and generous, but she was glad their house was not too close to their own. Their nearest neighbours were Deniel and his family on one side and Sébastien, Zélie and Francine on the other with their two girls. They were pleasant children but she

choice, a new branch, a new cell, and miles to go, and miles to go with no thought of sleep, our kith, the two-footed, once counted and weighed—eight miles of thread through a square inch of soil, and the next and the next,

of miles, thousands of miles, sugar and warnings, invocations and minerals, vibrating a language of electrical impulse, of fibres and food, resources and drought, danger and succour, hunger and plenty, trickling

particularly warmed to Alice, who, at fourteen, was awkward and unsure of herself, born during the Shift. It must have been a hard time for Zélie to be pregnant. She didn't like being around Claire. The old lady was bright and warm-hearted, but too talkative, especially about her husband and two sons. It was terrible, of course it was, but she'd lived a long life and had her daughters living with her, Brigitte and Diane both doting on her, and her youngest, Christophe, was a fine potter with a talented partner, Enora, and their three healthy, bright children. Really, she didn't want to hear Claire's story over and over again. There were others in the hamlet who'd lost husbands and sons, mostly sons, who, mercifully didn't tell her all the details at every opportunity. And Viola—only forty—she'd been separated from her mother young, lost her partner before her baby was born… She could see Viola's grief, as she could see Deniel's for his wife, but they didn't push it at her. Sometimes someone would bluntly ask her or Catherine what had

for once upon forever there was and is and always will be one fibre, another… and once, before memory, a filament said—let there be branching, decision was made and we saw it was good, mycelia knowing that there's always a

dialects of healing and flow. listen. voices filament through hyphae, stories of memory, of transformation, decisions throbbing underfoot, rising through every green thing, every flower and leaf, each blade of grass. and they

happened to them before they arrived at the village. She'd walked away once when Cloé asked and had been pursued by the noisy girl's mother, Marie-Claude, telling her how rude she'd been, how upset Cloé was. She'd wanted to shout back, let a torrent of memories gush out to scald the stupid woman, but she'd only told Marie-Claude to please tell her daughter she'd meant no offense. She held the tea close for a moment, closed her eyes and took a long draught. Rose. There were rose petals in the blend, cool and kind, wrapping her heart with their scent and… Rose, she said to the breeze. That was my wife's middle name. She opened her eyes and Deniel was standing in front of her, grey-skinned, his eyes yellow and with a look in them that she hadn't seen before, something… Sorry, I… No. Don't apologise. I intruded. It's good to get a moment alone at events like this, isn't it? She nodded, studying him. His posture had changed, not the illness, something internal that she couldn't name. So your wife was Elisabeth Rose? she asked. She was, he said, though

expanding in every dimension, many and one, filling space and time. we are immortals sensing each movement of wind-whispered grass, alive to each hoofstep of deer, scuttle of mole, each paw weight compressing, on and on, listened—those who were called, came by sea and by land, by train or on foot, for it seemed enough to come to the forest, to live.

I always knew her simply as Beth. My daughter was simply Rose, she told him. She was tiny when she was born—it had seemed enough—Rose—a tiny word for a tiny baby. She didn't add a tiny being whose presence had filled her life. He nodded and she felt the magnitude of his understanding and her own for him, his love, his resolution. Enough, he echoed quietly, nodding. She nodded in return, understanding him, put down her cup and walked across the road, descending the steep slope into the forest.

electric with impulse, every shade of vibration rhythming through earth, through roots, sap and bark, through leaf, flower… each pulse a word, each word a beat of a sentence, of flow, connecting us cell to cell, extending,

Chapter 4

She banged on the gong again. The temperature was climbing and they'd need to shelter in the afternoon before returning for the feast. Alex would stay at L'Autre Rive to periodically check on the boar and Anna and Joëlle would be back early to roast spatchcocked chickens. She watched people wandering back towards their homes. She gazed down the road towards Huelgoat and back towards the village, listening. The sounds of children and a couple of dogs, relatives of Fragan, deerhounds who helped keep them fed, someone singing as she walked, but no sound of the forager's cart. Would he pass through today? She shook herself and breathed deeply, closing her eyes as she inhaled the green of the forest into her lungs, an image of Hugo springing to mind—

I have a question for you. He rarely looked uneasy and she

was tempted to string this out like a cat with her prey. Grow up, she'd told herself. Out loud she'd simply said, Yes. He looked puzzled. Yes? She grinned, her freckled face pink, grey-blue eyes crinkled with laughter. How do you know what I was going to ask you? Did someone… I mean… Yes, someone told me. Who? She walked across the room and reached her arms around his neck. You, you clot. Not in words, of course, but I'm not blind. He put his arms around her waist. And you said yes? Yes to… All of it, Hugo Sándor. Absolutely all of it.

It was a few days before Winter Solstice when they set up her room on the middle floor of L'Autre Rive as their new bedroom overlooking the garden and forest at the edge of the hamlet. His bedroom (the smallest room on the attic floor) would become Hugo's study, always piled with drifts of books and papers, musical instruments, oracle cards, a messy haven from Viola's tidying. Her books, a couple of

in the forest is a world and the world is life

precious novels and the herbals she'd lugged in her back-sac from Ireland, together with the herb books that Isabelle had given her from the stock left behind in L'Autre Rive, and personal additions that Isabelle had treasured for years but insisted on gifting her, would stay on the bookshelves in what had once been the café and now was their library and living room, dining and making room, separated from the outer part of the kitchen, with its work surfaces and sinks, only by the L-shaped counter, and housing two wood-fired stoves that Isabelle had installed when she moved to the cold, damp hamlet, not knowing how essential they would become in the years after electricity was no longer there to spark boilers. Winter Solstice to Spring Equinox was a little over twelve weeks, and in those weeks nowhere was remote enough to be unaware of the Bane leaping across the world, the news of mounting death tolls crashing into their consciousness daily There had been other pandemics, viral influenzas or SARS or, further back, smallpox, or bacterial

in the earth are words and the words are health

outbreaks like the bubonic plague that killed whole swathes of populations. In the pandemics of the twentieth and twenty-first century the numbers of deaths had been appalling, though the percentages of deaths worldwide had been tiny compared to some of the estimates of the mediaeval losses. The novel strain of E.coli bacteria that struck in the Spring of 2049, more transmissible than anything that had come before it, heavily targeting the more susceptible immune systems of men in its death toll, was antibiotic resistant. It swept through the Americas from its epicentre in Louisiana, swiftly crossing continents east and west. But still they continued to cling to a desperate belief that their rural isolation and robust good health would see them through, or at least to tell each other it would. The three of them made endless supplies of cider vinegars infused with varying combinations of thyme, rosemary, basil, coriander, sage, spearmint and fennel, persuaded everyone in the hamlet and beyond to eat copious amounts of garlic and include juniper and ginger in their diets. They made supplies of oregano and liquorice root tinctures in preparation for illness and encouraged people to take tinctures and teas that would support their immunity. Isabelle's friends, Michel and Béa, organised an emergency committee and soon the whole hamlet had agreed that none of them would travel, not even to the nearest town of Huelgoat for shopping. All foods and medicines would be bought online and delivered to the most isolated house at the far side of the village. It was occupied by their daughter Ghislaine, her husband Rémy and their two young girls, but the family agreed to move in with Michel and Béa so that the house would be empty—a large sign directing the delivery people to the weather-proofed and empty wood store at the side of the building. Still death came. Beth was the first to die, on a sweltering July day. Deniel and Alex posted a notice on their door and asked for food to be left at a safe distance. It was clear from the note, brief as it was, that

in the earth are words and the words are health

neither of them expected to live. They would bury Beth at night, out beyond the village. The rest of the community met in the far field the next day—standing apart, agreeing they would all lock their doors. Each house would have a time to walk in the forest. One person from each home would collect their share of each delivery at an agreed time, including disinfected bottles of tinctures and teas packed in boiled tins. Michel and Rémy's deaths followed within a week of Beth. Béa, Ghislaine and the little ones were too sick to collect provisions and Élodie's husband, Pierrick agreed to leave food and medicines at their door, posting a note and ringing the bell before sprinting away. He was the next to go, never knowing his grandson and namesake, born three years later. Claire and Marie-Claude lost their husbands on the same day, Marie-Claude's five-year old daughter dying the day after her father and two of Claire's sons in the same week. André, Jacques, Simone, Théo, Louis. The names would stay with her forever. And so it went on—Aimée's husband, Charles, Brigitte's husband, Gervais on the same day as his son, Pierre, Cynthia's twin and just turned ten. Enora and Noé's parents, Pascal and Gigi. Deniel and Alex posted a note on the delivery house that they would dig graves for those who needed it. A note should be left at their gate post. They would collect the wrapped body after dark and bury their neighbour with dignity. In September there was a week without a death, then another. They kept to their isolation. She felt like she held her breath for every moment of those weeks. The news from the world that came through Internet and radio, television and, once, a drive-by van with a loudhailer from the Mayor's office, was intended to instil fear. She clung to Hugo, counted the men still left, but knew none of them were immune. The whole of September without a new grave, then Alain got sick. It had seemed miraculous that he'd survived when his father was ill, but now they expected Élodie to lose her son, thirty-one, tall and strong, a woodworker with a gift for spinning stories. But Alain had the knack of miracles. The fever left him after three days, the cramps within a week. The exhaustion persisted and he had no appetite for a month, but he was alive. Sébastien and Zélie became ill but, like Alain, survived—fatigued, gaunt, alive. She knew she was pregnant even before she'd missed her period, but waited. No blood came. Should she tell Hugo? Should she let the baby grow safer before she gave him such hope? There was no more sickness that month, none as November got underway. By the end of November she was bursting to tell him the news, but perhaps it would make a Winter Solstice gift—news of a life in this year of death. She held her joy close, shaking him awake early on the morning of the Solstice. They held each other tight, crying and laughing, made love and cried some more before Hugo disappeared to make breakfast—a celebratory meal when they would tell Isabelle, but no one else for a while. At breakfast they drank warmed elderflower cordial with sparkling water and ate Isabelle's fresh-made croissants with the last of the Summer's strawberry jam. They exchanged small gifts—books, a painting that Isabelle had done of the two of them, working in secret from photographs they didn't know she had taken, a beautiful pen they gave Isabelle that had once belonged to Hugo's father, a thick woven scarf that she gave to Hugo— she had found it at a market last Winter and hidden it away for the future, glad now that she had kept it aside. Hugo gave her a silver pendant—an oval disc with the raised imprint of a violet in bloom. Simple and beautiful. Violet and rose—these were her companion plants, her name plants and familiars. After a year of fear and grief, here they were, smiling, replete and together. And she was pregnant, bursting with life. She hoped that in other homes in the hamlet there other moments like this being played out—that Marie-Claude and her daughter Cloé would be glad to be living with Marie-Claude's sister, Ghislaine, that Ghislaine would be glad of them too and of her daughters who had survived the Bane. And so the year turned and they leant into it full of hope. It was the second day of the year when Francine and Gaëlle-Anne arrived. They'd known the women in better days—distant neighbours in an even smaller hamlet about three kilometres down the road. Gaëlle-Anne was a weaver and Francine and her mother stabled horses while her father ran a small-holding. Of the five households in their tiny settlement, they were the only survivors, but the last death had been in early September and they had both been well through the Winter. They wrote this on notes, posting them to every house that might be inhabited, then waited in the far field. Deniel came and stood outside each house in turn, calling out that they should let the women move into the empty cottage on the top road, asking each house to call out their agreement. Only Claire dissented, but Christophe came to an upstairs window and called out that his mother had misspoke herself, that he and his sisters said yes. And so the women moved in and it was right that they did. And perhaps their coming had nothing to do with Hugo falling sick a week later, the last of the community to be taken by the Bane. Deniel and Alex buried Hugo under an oak tree he had loved and she and Isabelle sat by it for hours the next day, weeping and telling stories, silently wondering if they too would soon be sick, if the baby would live.

She became aware of someone calling her name and shook herself. You were a long way away. She smiled up at the forager sitting at the reins of his huge chestnut carthorse. Gwilherm, I was wondering if you might come by today. He grinned. Ah, so that's what had you in a reverie—thinking I might turn up? She patted Conker. No, I just wanted to see this beauty, she said, rubbing the horse's neck. Ha! Touché. She smiled again. I was lost in the past, she admitted. Birthdays will do that, he said, especially auspicious ones that fall on the Summer Solstice. Ah, so you're here for the food? Too right, he agreed, jumping down from the wagon. Just going to walk Conker up to the stable, get him settled with his beloved Francine, and then I might… just might, have something in the vardo of interest to birthday people. Wonderful, you're on. Do you want tea or cider when you get back? Hmm, tough choice, but I'd better start slow so it has to be tea, unless you've got one of those ginger bugs brewing—that has to be the most addictive drink without alcohol on the planet. She studied him for a moment, his easiness in his skin, the way he kept any conversation light. She knew he'd been in Quimper during the Bane and the Shift, that he'd seen more horror than they could imagine, tucked away in their hamlet, despite the trauma of losing so many loved ones. And yet the lightness about him didn't seem to be a mask, or not a false one. I think I can find you some ginger bug, she said. Go and stable Conker and we can get out of this sun.

smooth mallow and cool,
here there is iron for blood,
and your heart is held.

Chapter 5

She watched Gwilherm walk Conker around the left fork of the road and went inside, the cool of the building's stone welcoming her. Zoé and Alice had stayed with Lisette and she could hear the buzz of their voices from the floor above. Isabelle and Alex were sat at the table, a pot of tea steaming between them. Immunitea, Alex said, another one of my favourites—I think it's the hibiscus and ground ivy that I really taste, but they're all good. She smiled. They are. Gwilherm just arrived. He's taking Conker up to Francine. I promised him ginger bug. She walked round the counter to the pantry behind at the back of the building and removed the damp sacking from the cooling box that worked on evaporation. There were smaller zeer pots on the shelves to keep soon-to-be-used vegetables cool, though they struggled in the humidity of the forest. The bulk of supplies were dried and stored in barns or kept inside the

this is our body, fallen, extinguished, our litany of loss. you remember pandemics, fire, flood, war, disease. we remember ancestors. the trees that are extinct, a fragment of our body, the forest. the memorial of all animals, plants lost to the earth would be recited forever. these are a sliver of all that has gone,

diverse, given to succour, to solace and heal. we wither
alone, sicken in plantations. Rooted, we pass on wisdom,
generation to generation. When the world warmed, when
the rains thinned, we adapted, though some of us fell,

series of root cellars built across the hamlet. Today there
would be a series of nets and crates submerged in the fastest
running parts of the river, filled with drinks for the
evening—cider and elderflower champagne, vegetable
wines, jars of kombucha fermented from herbs, ginger bug
blends with lemon and honeyed peppermint. She savoured
the flavours in her imagination as she poured two large
glasses of the cool ginger for Gwilherm and herself.

Gwilherm stayed chatting to Francine as she welcomed
Conker, took off the harness. I'll take him down to the field
tomorrow early, she said. I don't think it'll get above thirty-
five today, but he's already done heavy work. The cool of the
stable and some good feed for this afternoon. And some
friends to catch up with, eh, Conker? The horse whinnied in
reply and he admired how Francine seemed to be part of the
horse's world in a way he would never feel, though he adored
Conker. He often had an urge to ask about her life before.
He knew she had arrived from a nearby hamlet with Gaëlle-

trees lost in the blink of time that is the last four decades in
Europe, one fragment of the globe. our dirge in memoriam.
Akamas Centaury (Centaurea akamantis), Allium iatrouinum,
Antirrhinum subbaeticum, Apid den Bermejo (Apium
bermejoi), Arran Service-tree (Sorbus pseudofennica),

though the litany of our lost was long and ever-expanding, we knew in our roots that there would be trees after storm and flood, after fire and plague, after ice age and warming. we have always returned, again and again. in

Anne during the last gasps of the Bane, that she had lost people as they all had. At some point she had fallen in love with Zélie. He found it hard to imagine a tiny rural settlement accepting a household of a married couple and the wife's female lover before the Shift, but he'd never sensed any unease about this in the local community. He supposed all their perspectives had changed, the Shift wasn't only the crumbling of financial institutions and corporations. It was as though they had moved to a different world with only a semblance of sameness on the surface of things—the houses that stood, the people forming relationships, the needs for food and shelter and love. Was life more real now—no longer a society of spectacle, masses living the lives of simulacra? Did that make it better? He sighed. There was too much loss, too much unspoken trauma. Surely they were all still performers trying to convince themselves as much as those around them that they were functional, even contented, a good deal of the time. And it wasn't even that

Astragalus cavanillesii, Avon Gorge Whitebeam (Sorbus avonensis), Azores Juniper (Juniperus brevifolia), Barbaricina Colombine (Aquilegia barbaricina), Berberis maderensis, Betula celtiberica, Betula klokovii, Brimeura duvigneaudii, Bryoxiphium madeirense, Buglosse Crépu (Anchusa crispa),

those days, before the humans were afflicted again, before

thrive in damp, shade, sun,
calm gut, soothe throat, cool fever,
my sap for your stings.

the performance was wholly false. After all, look at this day—the forest green and lovely, the village well-kept, everyone playing their part despite the sores that they could rub against on one another, the children growing up skilful and loved, a generation that would no doubt pick up their parents' sadness but hopefully not the full depth of it. Or didn't it work like that? He used to enjoy reading psychology articles online in a former lifetime, but they had blurred together over the years. Perhaps there were books at L'Autre Rive he could borrow. He said goodbye to Conker, asked Francine how the rest of the family were doing, thanked her and said he'd see them all later. He walked past Catherine and Émilie's cottage and noticed Catherine stood in the doorway. They were closed books, those two, but he liked them. There was an honesty to their refusal to tell their stories and, truthfully, he'd told little of his own tale to anybody—only the broadest brush strokes of those two years hiding out in a basement, eventually having to scout

Bully Tree (Sideroxylon marginatum), Bupleuro delle (Bupleurum elatum), Bupleuro di Marettimo (Bupleurum dianthifolium), Calligonum triste, Canary Islands Juniper (Juniperus cedrus), Canary Strawberry Tree (Arbutus canariensis), Canutillo del Teide (Silene nocteolens), Cardón

for more supplies in the devastated and still dangerous
streets. She looked anxious but he was unsure if she would
welcome questions. He waved a greeting. You haven't seen
Émilie? she asked. No, but I only got here maybe a quarter
of an hour ago. Just took Conker to the stable but everyone
seems to be indoors. She hasn't come back, Catherine said,
and he walked closer to the cottage. Where were you? We
went to L'Autre Rive to help with the preparations. We'd
been putting candles out on the tables, then the gong rang
and I realised she'd vanished. He found both the women
difficult to age. Late fifties, early sixties? Catherine was
perhaps the older but not by much—broader, less fragile-
looking than Émilie, both of them were competent and self-
contained. They grew crops and sometimes foraged with
Viola. They fermented drinks in the barn behind Deniel's
longère and could knit wonderful sweaters from any wool
he found, including old jumpers that they would unravel
and rework. Catherine tucked a strand of white hair behind

resilient and we will breathe the air clean, allow us to spread, forest marching across the land, and we'll create rain, cool the earth for all to enjoy again. healing ourselves we will heal the world. but they did not listen.

her ear and scanned the road towards the house where Élodie lived in the little gite attached to the larger house that contained Gilles and Véronique and their children... Maybe she went for a walk? Catherine nodded, Yes, but usually she'd say something. Well always, actually... I thought maybe she had come back ahead of me, but... She shrugged and lifted her palms to the sky. I'm just about to grab a drink at L'Autre Rive, but I could go and look for her. She shook her head. I'm sure I'm fretting over nothing and she wouldn't thank me for sending a search party. Thank you, though, that's very kind. He walked on to L'Autre Rive wondering about Catherine and Émilie. Was it concerning that Émilie had taken some time alone? It couldn't be more than an hour? Ah, you're back. I hope the ginger is still cool, Viola said as he walked in. I'm sure it will be wonderful. He took the proffered glass. Even more delicious than I remember, he said, stopping to relish the hot spice of the ginger against the cool of peppermint and sharpness of

Cornish Path Moss (Ditrichum cornubicum), Cretan Zelkova (Zelkova abelicea), Crimean Rowan (Sorbus tauricola), Cyprus Cedar (Cedrus brevifolia), Derbyshire Feather-moss (Thamnobryum angustifolium), Distichophyllum carinatum, Dracaena draco (Canary Islands dragon tree), Echinodium

warmth and ease dwell here,
spice to cleanse sugar from blood,
dissolving your pain

lemon, the undertone of honey just right. You're a genius with herbs, all of you, he said, raising his glass to the household. Isabelle put her hands together in a gesture of thanks. And I presume the delicious scent of boar out there is your work, he said to Alex. Me and assorted others, Alex replied, laughing. I'd probably best go and see if it needs turning, back in a moment. Sit down, Gwilherm, Isabelle instructed, tell us your news, tell us what treasures you have to trade with us. You're staying for the feast, of course? I am, and happy birthday—to both of you. He raised the last portion of the ginger and drank it down. I've got gifts as well as trades, but the trades can wait till tomorrow. I'll fetch the gifts from the vardo in a minute but I just met Catherine— apparently Émilie disappeared at the end of setting up the tables. She's probably just taken herself off for a walk, but Catherine seemed worried—said she would normally let her know. She didn't want me to go and look but she was more unsettled than I've seen her. I saw Émilie when I went

spoke of managing forests, cut down our elders,
repositories of wisdom. unheeding, they saw us only as
stores of carbon, useful alive, more useful dead. when the
grey wolf returned we thrilled to the balance the apex

upstairs to rest, Isabelle put in. Lisette gave me my marching
orders so I went up to read for a while. I was watching all the
activity in the garden and noticed Émilie—I often wonder
if it's good for those two to keep all their secrets so close, but
perhaps it is. Sometimes I think we brutalise others telling
our past traumas, but it's a hard one to balance—stories
have to be processed, of course, and some stories need
witnesses. We're story-telling animals, after all. Even tales of
horror can be instructive, important to keep alive. Isabelle
stopped—Anyway, Émilie looked up as though she knew I
was watching her and I turned back into my room, so it's
not much to report, except that she seemed fine. I'm sure
she's just gone for a walk, Gwilherm agreed, and Catherine
was certain she wouldn't appreciate being searched for, so I
suppose there's not much we can do. I could pop back to the
cottage in a couple of hours and see if she's home yet, but I
don't want to add stress to what's probably nothing. Viola
agreed. Unless you have anything for them? I mean if you

torrenticola, Gyrocaryum oppositifolium, Harz' Mehlbeere
(Sorbus harziana), Heberdenia excelsa, Helianthemum
guerrae, Hieracium lucidum, Horstrissea dolinicola, Jaramago
de Alboran (Diplotaxis siettiana), Jasione mansanetiana,
Kythrean Sage (Salvia veneris), Lamyropsis microcephala,

predator brings, but the humans, emerging from a blight that had infested their world could only think of more management and plans. leave us alone, we continued to cry. we have the wisdom to heal ourselves, to heal the

had another reason to go there. He pursed his lips—a few balls of wool, not much, and I usually take things to the gather-hall so it might seem a bit odd… I think you're right, she said. Let's wait. Catherine will ask for help if she needs it and Émilie knows the forest as well as any of us. This is always a strange day—festivals bring back memories. In any case, I'm sure someone mentioned gifts. He watched the animation of her face as she spoke. In the ten years he'd known her the deep russet of her hair had faded to a sandy bronze, but she looked otherwise unchanged. Sometimes he had a sense that he was coming to know her, that with each visit he understood a little more, but there was a reserve in her, deeper than Catherine's and Émilie's—and different in quality—something more fundamental than guarding a story. She rarely appeared still when others were around—always making teas or tinctures, out foraging or gardening, cooking or helping someone, but he knew that alone, she would sit in the forest for hours or hole up in her room to

Larkspur (Delphinium iris), Ligusticum huteri, Limonium strictissimum, Lithodora nitida, Llangollen Whitebeam (Sorbus cuneifolia), Llanthony Whitebeam (Sorbus stenophylla), Lonicera karataviensis, Lunetiere de Rotges (Biscutella rotgesii), Lysimachia minoricensis, Maltase Cliff-

lives that teem on the earth, we will share the sky-rivers
dark crone's Solstice froth,
proof against fever, burns, wounds,
blossoming healing

write or read, losing all track of time. She had a way of going inside herself that could be unnerving. He'd heard Lisette call it a gift for oblivion, though not with approval. I wonder if you have any psychology books in your library? he said. I'd love to borrow some if you have. She laughed. Well, that's an interesting non sequitur to my rude request for presents, she said, but yes—there are quite a few. He smiled. Sorry, that was more than a bit random. And your prompting wasn't rude. Let me go and get them. He got up, flustered, glad to go out to the wagon. Inside, he perched for a while on the faded and threadbare pink of the little seat nestled next to the green-tiled nook that housed the stove, a battered kettle on top, storage hooks for pans above. At the back, under the bed, were cupboards, their gilt, red and green paintings of roses chipped and bleached, but the wood still sound. Drawers ran down one side of the wagon towards another battered seat, both of them built over more storage areas. Not an inch of the vardo was wasted so that he

we create to cool and hydrate our leaves, our bodies, our rooted brains. we will give you healing and life. instead they cleared a swathe through our body. planted Douglas firs in rows. shutting out light. talked of biomass value.

could travel from home with everything he needed and room to stash his finds. As much as he appreciated the gite that had become home a decade ago, he loved the snugness of the vardo's space—it's intimacy, the feeling of being held. He'd briefly struck up a relationship with Caroline a few years ago. She was seven years younger and the sex had been frequent and robust, as had the arguments, which he'd had no taste for. He'd felt like he was living in the funnel of the tornado, not the still eye of the storm. It had made him feel more alone than ever and she was unsurprised when he finally mustered the courage to tell her that it wasn't working. Unsurprised but bitter. You should give Nicole a try, she'd said and he hadn't known how to respond to the sour joke of being offered her sister. Or one of the noisy girls. They're fifteen years younger than me! he'd blurted. Thirteen—Cynthia would only be thirteen years younger. And Hugo was way more ancient than Viola. No one seemed to find that creepy. He felt an argument gathering

Mehlbeere (Sorbus meierottii), Minuartia dirphya, Moehringia fontqueri, Morris Squill (Scilla morrisii), Myrica rivas-martinezii, Narcissus gaditanus, Narcissus lusitanicus, Narcissus nevadensis, Narcissus willkommii, Naufraga balearica, Nees' Hornwort (Anthoceros neesii), No Parking

how soon they could clear-fell their assets, our screams
went unheard year after year, and when the slaughter and
interference ceased, we imagined that those who could
hear us had finally held sway, but it was not human

and wanted to extricate himself, but they were in the vardo.
I just meant it's not... I'm not looking... She threw her
hands in the air. Whatever. The shagging was fine while it
lasted. It's not like I imagined us becoming a couple. She'd
left and he'd felt guilty that he was so relieved, that he'd
upset her and then let her go like that, but he felt more
exhaustion than anything else. It was early in the evening,
only a little after six, and he'd curled onto the bed under its
red roof, the paint only peeling slightly, and slept till seven
the next morning, waking with the feeling that he'd escaped
something dark and consuming. Solstices! he said out loud
into the hot, still air of the wagon. These times always stirred
memories. He opened a drawer under the seat beside the
stove and pulled out two gifts. He'd wrapped them in old
bits of fabric that no doubt would find their way to one of
Enora or Gaëlle-Anne's projects, both of them ingenious
with any textile. Back indoors, he placed the packages on
the table and sat down. The group had grown, Lisette and

Tree (Sorbus admonitor), Nuragica Columbine (Aquilegia
nuragica), Ochyraea tatrensis, Orthotrichum handiense,
Pleiomeris canariensis, Polygala helenae, Polygala sinisica,
Pyrus anatolica, Radula jonesii, Rhamnus integrifolia, Riccia
atlantica, Salix canariensis, Salix xanthicola, Salviablanca de

76

compassion or wisdom that had changed. once again they

tart sun heart easer,
acid for kidneys, bright oil,
to lift the spirit.

two of her friends standing to watch the small ceremony, and Alex, back in from turning the roast. Gwilherm handed the gift in dark blue fabric to Isabelle. How kind, she said, untying the string. Inside was a silk scarf, pale blue, the dye looking like water along its shimmering length. It's exquisite, Isabelle said softly. Where on earth did you find it? I… Well, actually, I… I've had it for a while. It belonged to my mother. Oh, Gwilherm. I'm honoured, but really… I mean are you sure you want… It's much more sad that it's never worn, he said. I didn't take a lot of stuff when I left the house. I wasn't sure I'd live—both my parents died so quickly, so it felt useless to try to carry much, but there were some things that—I suppose they seemed part of them— so… Anyway, I realised it's been years since I've taken it out and looked at it. I'd like it to be used. Isabelle put a hand on Gwilherm's arm—It will be. Thank you. It's beautiful. She wrapped it elegantly around her neck and smiled at everyone. The second package, it's covering a soft green with

Doramas (Sideritis discolor), Saponaria jagelii, Sardinian Currant (Ribes sardoum), Scapania sphaerifera, Schuwerk Mehlbeere (Sorbus schuwerkiorum), Sea Marigold (Calendula maritima), Serbian Spruce (Picea omorika), Ship Rock Whitebeam (Sorbus parviloba), Shrubby Buckwheat

were dying, and in greater numbers than ever before, one who loved us, who knew how to listen, was buried beneath the oldest oak, his grave watered with tears and the rain we made, those who believed we existed to be managed

fine yellow stripes, was bulkier, oddly shaped. He handed it to Viola and for a moment she held his gaze so that he had a sensation of being seen into. And then she was untying the knots, Lisette affectionately mocking as she struggled with them. Mezaluna, Viola said, and this—they're superb. The first knife was a half moon blade, a dark wooden handle at each end so that the user could rock it back and forth to chop herbs finely. Why mezaluna? Zoé asked. It's Italian for half moon, Lisette answered for her mother. Nice! The other was a steel sickle, perhaps eight inches long. It's very sharp, Gwilherm cautioned. Good, Viola returned. She placed the handle in her palm, a little shorter than the blade, its smooth, rounded length fitted well—a foraging tool of usefulness and beauty. They're amazing finds. It was on a long forage, he said. A house I came across that was untouched. Strange place—I'll tell you the story some time.

He had thought he was in a dream. He'd had a terrible head

(Atraphaxis muschketowi), Sibiraea tianschanica, Sicilian Fir (Abies nebrodensis), Silene de Ifac (Silene hifacensis), Silene marizii, Silene orphanidis, Solenanthus reverchonii, Sorbus barrandienica, Sorbus busambarensis, Sorbus cucullifera, Sorbus milensis, Sorbus moravica, Sorbus pauca, Sorbus

and cleared, our bodies not allowed to return to the soil, but sold, ceased to visit with their tools and the machines that compacted the soil, crushing roots, constricting mycelia, ceased to torment us. such a little time we have

cold, or something worse while travelling, and had gone off route without even noticing. It was the most scared he'd been in years. There were no buildings around and he'd lost all bearings. The area was wooded and he'd pulled in to what looked like no more than an old passing point but there was something about the way the hedge was growing—as though branches had been pulled and trained, though not recently. He might not have noticed if he hadn't been a little delirious, but he started pulling at the foliage. There seemed to be a driveway beyond so he got out tools and kept tunnelling through the shrubs. He had no idea how long he'd worked, but eventually he saw the rutted drive. He took the wagon through and spent as long, perhaps longer, covering his tracks, reconstructing some kind of hedge. The lane went on and on and he'd begun to think it led nowhere, but then he turned a corner and saw the house in the dip— a big square manor. He left the vardo and crept towards it, but it was clearly deserted so he retraced his steps and

portae-bohemicae, Sorbus rhodanthera, Sorbus spectans, Sorbus thayensis, Sorbus tobani, Spiraeanthus schrenkianus, Star Thistle (Centaurea corensis), Stonecress (Aethionema retsina), Succisella andreae-molinae, Teucrium balthazaris, Thin-Leaved Whitebeam (Sorbus leptophylla), Troodos

been free, but we feel the joy of it in the water that is our
breathe slowly and deep,
ease sickness, pain and gut
and so digest life.

walked Conker in. The door was locked but he'd managed
to jemmy it, terrified of what he'd find inside. There were a
couple of bodies in a bedroom—or rather a collection of
teeth, bones and hair in one of the beds. The house hadn't
been touched. Everything was as they left it the night they
went to bed together and didn't wake up. Part of him
wanted to leave it alone, but he was feverish and exhausted
so slept in the big living room downstairs. When he woke
the fever had broken. He was beyond tired, even after
sleeping, but not feeling sick. He cooked in the vardo and
then began going through the place for the most useful
things he could carry. He navigated his way out the next day,
took home the haul, then turned round and went back to
the manor. It had given him a lot of trades, but he'd emptied
it of the useful finds over the next visits. He doubted there
would ever be another find like it. The kitchen had once
been beautiful, drawers of high quality kitchen knives, pots
displayed on enamel stands or hung over the large range

Rockcress (Arabis kennedyae), Twin Cliffs Whitebeam
(Sorbus eminentoides), Urartuan Milkwort (Polygala urartu),
White's Whitebeam (Sorbus whiteana), Würzburger
Mehlbeere (Sorbus herbipolitana), Yesquera Amarilla
(Helichrysum gossypinum), Yesquera Roja (Helichrysum

blood, in our heartwood and rooting brains. each year, the names of those extinct for all time grows less, the endangered breathe another year, another, the critical *stagger on rejoicing*, this is our body, the forest.

cooker—some of them now in Viola's kitchen or other houses in the hamlets he visited, but there were things he'd kept aside… not sure why he was doing so—only that they seemed too special to trade straight away.

How long ago was it? Viola asked. Two years come Autumn. He didn't say that he'd returned almost immediately and then three more times at monthly intervals on the dark moons of Autumn and Winter, something superstitious warning him to go when he was least likely to be noticed, even in so remote a place. Viola held the knives, one in each palm, feeling their weight. Thank you, she said. They'll get lots of use. Thank you.

monogynum), Yorkshire Feather-moss (Thamnobryum cataractarum), Zelkova sicula. this is our body, extinguished, fallen, our litany of loss.

how wash-away-flow-away-sluice-lap-trickle-flood how river feels rising how dew feels dissolving on leaf how rain feels baptising stem how moisture feels soaking earth roots pooling in flower sliding down bud how snow melt

Chapter 6

She washed dishes in the kitchen, passing them to Lisette to dry. Alex had gone back to check on the boar and Zoé and Alice had returned to their homes for a few hours before the party began. Lisette had shooed Isabelle to her room to rest some more, arguing it would be a long night and since the moon had only recently been full, Isabelle wouldn't have slept well for the last few nights. Gwilherm had gone to rest in the spare room that had once been Hugo's study, cooler than his wooden vardo, and had taken a small stack of psychology books with him to browse. She'd wanted to ask him more about the deserted manor house—Where was it? Had he found the bodies of the people who lived there or had they left? Had he gone back more than once? Why had it stood untouched for so long? So many stories there. But she liked how Gwilherm used his stories sparingly. He wasn't a closed person—far from it, but he wasn't... a performer?

at forest nerves... unconscious consciousness... reaching... turning... cells... branch-turn-reach... turn-reach-branch... unselfconscious shout of joy... nerve-cells... being... reach-branch-turn... this is how...

Was that the right word? Not quite. He was
undemonstrative but there was a clarity to him. Her
daughter had a similar clarity, but was more outspoken. It
was these differences that she looked for in people when
they came for help from the herbs. There was never a
standard blend for a standard complaint, which was what
made the remedies endlessly fascinating, this tripartite of
herbs, suppliant and herbalist was never the same twice and
always there was more to learn. She knew Isabelle felt the
same, though had always favoured a background role. She
used to joke with Hugo that she would only ever be the
herbalist's assistant, yet she'd studied in so many countries
and languages, drinking in the wisdom of Oisín in
Brocéliande, spending time with a scholar of Ibn Al-Wâfid
of Toledo, an alchemical herbalist who had lived at the court
of Princess Casilda's father, Alaman, in the last years of
Moorish rule, and wrote great works on simples and sleep,
curing so many diseases, always working with diet before

how heat shocks how plasma membranes how proteins
fold how thirsting how mutations how leaf death how cell
death thirsting dry-parched how heat-waved open
channels calcium channels how signal metabolites

adding the simplest of herbs. Isabelle's teacher, Aafiq Al-
Birzali, ran a tiny halal restaurant on the corner of Calle
Ciudad and Calle de San Marcos, Tulaytula—
remembrance, his life devoted to remembering and passing
on the work of his two mentors who had lived a thousand
years before—Ibn Al-Wâfid and Ibn Sina, the philosopher
and healer commonly known as Avicenna. Ibn Al-Wâfid had
written *Kitab al-adwiya al-mufrada*, never published in
Arabic but Al-Birzali had the fragmentary Latin translation,
Liber de medicamentis simplicibus, and another in Catalan, as
well as translations of Al-Wâfid's pharmacopeia, sometimes
known as *al-wisada fi'l-tib*—book of the pillow on
medicine, though more probably, if less poetically, its true
title was *Kitab al-Rashad fi 'l-tibb*—guide to medicine.
Isabelle still had books of notes she had made during her
work with Al-Birzali. Later, she'd acquired English copies of
the first two books of Avicenna's five volume tome, *The
Qanûn fi't-tibb*—his *Canon of Medicine*. They stood on the

relate-reach-connect-branch-turn... how the forest...
unselfconscious... branch-connect-turn-reach-relate...
how the... shout... turn–branch-relate-connect-reach...
of joy... becomes... connect-turn-reach-branch-relate...

chaperones   how—carotenoids   glutathione   proline
glycine   betaine   rehalose—protect   how   resolubalise
proteins   how   sense   and   signal   sense   and   signal
transcribing genes how block and defend how prime and

herbal shelves in the library at L'Autre Rive. Isabelle had
moved back to Paris after Toledo, but continued to travel
often, studying in rural Bulgaria, in Prague, and at a herbal
farm in the Var, high in the Provence Alps, where the hyssop
had a unique chemotype and lavender scented the valley.
She had passed all this on to herself and Hugo, but Isabelle's
true apprentice was Lisette. She caught her daughter's eye as
she handed her the last dish to dry and they smiled, Lisette
not needing to mention how she'd been miles away, lost in
her own thoughts as so often. She adored her daughter and
knew herself loved in return—the bond was fierce and
unassailable, but when it came to teaching, Isabelle and
Lisette had a rapport that ran deep, perhaps as deep as the
centuries of learning they pored over together.

Lisette put away the last dry cup and hung the cloth. I'm
off to Zoé's, she said. I'll be back in plenty of time for
heating the soups and… I'm sure you will, Viola agreed. Go
and do whatever the two of you are up to. Lisette grinned.

nerve-cells… being… joy… reach-relate-turn-connect-
branch…   shout   of…   unconscious   consciousness…
being…   turn-relate-reach-branch-listen-connect…   of
joy… unselfconscious shout… becoming… at forest…

No spoilers. And you should go and read or write or do
something you want to do while it's quiet. I'll let Alex know
to make himself drinks while he's here. She watched her
mother mulling over something before she said, I did
wonder about… No, she interrupted. You don't need to go
and check on Deniel or go and see if Émilie is back home or
anything else you might be thinking. Go read a book, go
daydream… go relax if you can remember how to do that.
Viola laughed. Yes, Mum, Viola quipped, hugging her
before heading upstairs. She stopped by the roast to tell Alex
the kitchen was all his. Noé had promised to come and take
over mid-afternoon so he'd be away soon too, but he would
let Noé know to make himself at home. She took the fork to
the lane that led to Zoé's house, a long oblong with a gite at
one end where Zoé's grandmother lived. Her mother,
Véronique, took on the teaching for the hamlet's children
with her brother, Alain. Both of them were natural
storytellers and good musicians. Gilles, Zoé's dad, led the

sluice-lap-trickle-flood… how light quenches hunger,
how greening light satiates how sucking soil minerals how
bland nitrogen how acrid-garlic phosphorous bitter-sweet
as lead bursts umami how potassium bitters metal-salt

hunting and fishing parties, always accompanied by the
noisy girls, who were quiet and stealthy when they were on
an expedition. Between their houses were two barns, one for
preserving and one for salting. She wondered if all hamlets
worked as well as theirs. In Winter the food could become
repetitive and there had been a couple of Winters when they
had needed to watch the provisions carefully, but she'd never
felt genuinely hungry. She knew from Isabelle that it was
harder in Ireland where her grandmother, Saoirse, lived. The
houses around Reagh were more spread out, but there was a
community living in what had once been the local pub who
traded meat for the fish she caught and some of the
vegetables she grew and, like her mother, she was a gifted
herbalist so they would always make sure she was safe. She'd
been told so much about the time before the Shift, much of
it sounding like fantasy —money instead of trading or gifts,
people working in buildings that were built for nothing else,
types of communication that sounded more magical than

branch-relate-turn-listen… listen-… at forest… turn…
being… relate-… shout… connect-… of… reach-…
joy… becoming… branch… unselfconscious… nerve-
… how the… cells… forest… how the forest…

how calcium salty-chalk-sours magnesium tart-metals iron rancids taste of blood how water slakes sour fizz of carbon dioxide, sugars the day, how respiring waste oxygen lightens sap how light quenches hunger... how

the stories of the Otherworld Alain, Hervé and Véronique told. Viola had been born into an increasingly digital world—virtual and augmented reality—she knew the words but the leap of imagination stumped her. It had been a world of rapidly growing inequalities—those with the most digital access and most money living radically different lives than those who struggled to pay for rent, heating or food. It was a world without privacy, something she couldn't fathom at all—companies, banks and governments constantly gathering information, cameras in the streets—a world of products that apparently included the people. A world of mass information, much of it false or contorted, keeping people afraid and divided. The Bane had taken so many, the father she had never known among them, more men than women, more old than young, though the very young had also been vulnerable. It came in waves—though the pulses eased more quickly away from the cities. Places with higher populations, numbers she couldn't conceive of, where more

becomes... listen... listen... the unselfconscious... connect... connect... shout... reach... reach... of... branch... branch... joy... relate... relate... being... turn... turn... at forest... at for... ner... est ves...

light rhythms how differentiate light and shadow how
myriad colours perceived how ultraviolet to infrared
vision how see direction of light sense dark days and light
winter and summer seeing the length of days how

people than she would ever meet in her lifetime might live
in a single tower block, suffered wave after wave—for almost
two years—and the body counts added to other diseases.
Public services crumbled rapidly, banks closed and
communication faltered. And in between the rounds of
death, and afterwards, there was human savagery. Zoé said
her uncle Alain's partner, Hervé, and his sister Julie, escaped
from one of those places. They'd been twenty-four and
nineteen when they left a place called Poitiers, two years
after the Bane began, but before the Shift had finally ground
to a halt. There had still been some Internet sites and
sometimes a phone signal as they set out to walk hundreds
of kilometres, constantly hiding, half-starved and terrified.
Zoé said Hervé wouldn't say much about what had
happened in Poitiers or about the walk, which had
meandered, sometimes coming to a halt for a while. But
occasionally bits of the story would leak out. It had been
over six months before they arrived at Kerkoad, gaunt and

uncon... reach scious... ing... con... turn... scious...
cells... ness... ing... bran... turn... ch... rea... turn...
ch... unself... rea... con... ch... shout... bran... scious
ch... of... ner...ve joy... cells... be... reach... ing

phytochrome signals shortening nights, calls leaf and
bloom how absorb blue light rhythming day circadian
how red light far-red light senses how sight flows
unimaged how light rhythms... how wind and rain hail

exhausted. They moved into an empty house that stood
alone in the field opposite the Gite d'Artus where Ghislaine
and her family lived. Alain and Hervé lived in that house
now, but it had been a few years before they became a
couple—the year after Julie and Noé got together, which
must have been 2056. In the years between, Alain had
experimented with not being gay by trying to maintain a
relationship with her mother. She'd liked Alain when she
was little, still did. He was always patient with her, kind and
full of stories, but even as a six-year-old she sensed that he
and Viola were an awkward combination. Alain was full of
emotion. He talked a lot and wanted to be talked to. She
hadn't been able to figure out why he had chosen her
taciturn mother as a partner. He'd also wanted a lot of
reassurance—needed to know everything about Viola's day,
would ask what Viola was thinking. She could feel her
mother's claustrophobia when Alain asked questions,
wanting to share her thoughts. How had Viola ever got into

bran... chturn... thi... sis... branhow... chturn...
conrea... chnect... thisis... turcon... renect... nach...
braho... nch... wuns... elfcon... scioust... his...
recon... achnect... braturn... ncshou... istof...

and sleet are felt how touch stresses how scream being eaten feel each insect forager deer how wind rain hail and sleet are felt... how listen for water underground knowing its fluid beat how roots travel towards moisture how sense

such a relationship? Her mother was so private, so seemingly self-sufficient, though she knew that Viola was more sensitive than she appeared. She imagined that Viola had thought she could help Alain, didn't want to hurt his feelings by turning him down, but the result was short and messy and her mother had not had a relationship since. Not that there were opportunities. Every man in the hamlet was with someone else except for Deniel, who was old and sick. Perhaps those of her own generation wouldn't be able to stay indefinitely in the cradle of this safe place if they wanted to have relationships or families one day. Sometimes she wondered if the noisy girls would eventually leave in search of something more. They all had mothers in the village, but still... Was Viola happy alone? She still missed Hugo, who had been an extraordinary person. She was certain of this not only because her mother had loved him so much but because Isabelle said so. But otherwise Viola seemed more than content, though unable to say no to the demands of

conhow... nectbran... turnch... jore acunch... yons... cious... reth... islat... ise... recac... honnect... brarn... nchtu... tho... whe... foruns... estelf... bracon... scinch... cous... tonn... ecturn... re-re... achlate... how vibration of caterpillar beetle releasing pesticides how tropism how listen for water... how vibrate-sussurate-sing-tinkle-drum-fizz how moss ticks to each raindrop dewdrop how each plant leaf flower timpanies a different

others, unable to admit that no-one can save someone else. She hoped today would be a good day for her mother, despite all the memories that were clearly surfacing. She'd obviously been thrilled with the gift Gwilherm had brought, as had Isabelle with hers. She hoped her own gift would be as appreciated, if less tangible. She knocked lightly on Zoé's door and Pierrick opened it. Zoé's just getting ready, he told her. Come in. She stood in the kitchen, cool after being in the sun's glare. Zoé came into the room carrying a violin case and Véronique called through to have a good afternoon practising. They set off across the goat field towards Alice's house, where she lived with her dad, two mums and younger sister. She was glad to have Zoé and Alice as friends, though sometimes Alice's diffidence annoyed Zoé. They walked past Catherine and Émilie's cottage and she noticed Catherine standing by the window. Looks like Émilie hasn't come home yet, she said to Zoé, telling her how Gwilherm had met Catherine earlier and she was worried that Émilie was

the... shout... becoming... branch-connect-relate-listen-turn-reach... is how the... unselfconscious... conscious forest... being... reach-listen-relate-turn-connect-branch... the shout of... nerve-cells... joy...

tune how storm and shower drum a million registers how a branch susurrates wind creaks dryness how sap fizzes ultrasonic how leaves tinkle whole trees vibrate song how vibrate-susurrate-sing-tinkle-drum-fizz how taste-hear-

missing. She'll just have gone for a walk, won't she? Zoé said. People worry too much. They walked around the barn in front of Alice's long L-shaped house, past the stables and into the courtyard. Alice emerged before they reached the door, carrying her flute case, and they went into the barn together. For Isabelle she had a small note book, constructed from rag paper that she had made out of scraps of fabric donated by Gaëlle-Anne and Enora. But for her mother she had written a song. She'd sung in a group often, all through her childhood, and sung for herself, often when she was out walking, but she had never performed as a solo voice to an audience. She'd learned how to read and write music from Véronique and Alain, like all the children and young people of the hamlet, but it was the first time she'd put a song together in this way. Zoé and Alice had been eager to help, though Alice was more nervous about the performance. Still, they sounded good together—violin, flute and voice. Véronique had listened to their last rehearsal and been full

becoming... connect-reach-branch-relate-turn-listen... listen-... at forest... turn... being... relate-... shout... connect-... of... reach-... joy... becoming... branch... unselfconscious... nerve-... how the... cells... forest...

scent-feel-see-listen-sense how wash-away-flow-away-sluice-lap-trickle-flood how light quenches hunger how light rhythms how wind and rain hail and sleet are felt how sing how sing how sing sing sing

of praise, but she still wondered about such an amorphous gift. Should she have thought of something that Viola could keep, something physical for a fortieth birthday? She was amused at her own desire to please, something that she'd normally associate with her mother rather than herself. And anyway, it was too late to change her mind now. They began the song and she heard her voice as though listening to someone else—clear and agile over the haunting melody of Alice's flute and the mellow tone of Zoé's violin. She relaxed into the piece. Yes, this was exactly the right gift for Viola.

how the forest... becomes... listen... listen... the unselfconscious... connect... connect... shout... reach... reach... of... branch... branch... joy... relate... relate... being... turn... turn... at forest listen-relate...

we are fragments of exploded stars

Chapter 7

She put down the book, stood and stretched. From her window she could see the garden set with tables, cooking areas, gazebos and awnings, the fire dish they would gather around in the last light of this longest day to thank the earth for life—the celebration of Alban Hefin. The house was still. Perhaps Gwilherm had fallen asleep over the psychology books and Isabelle was resting, or they might be quietly reading above her. Lisette had gone out, full of some secret that lit her from within, and Noé, who must have taken over from Alex, was tending to the boar. Everything that was needful was done, only the chickens to roast, dishes to heat as others arrived from around the hamlet. Forty. Age was such a strange thing… Part of her felt she had lived forever, another part was the young woman who had arrived on the ferry eighteen years ago. She sat on the bed, fingering the well-read book, one of Isabelle's favourites. It had seemed

our bodies are the earth

we are bodies composed of light eaten

like the right day to take it off the shelf, a day of memories. She opened the page of *À la recherche du temps perdu* at the point she had been reading—*The places we have known do not belong solely to the world of space in which we situate them for our greater convenience. They were only a thin slice among contiguous impressions which formed our life at the time: the memory of a certain image is but regret for a certain moment: and houses, roads, avenues are as fleeting, alas, as the years.* But for Proust this melancholy and fragility of memory was not what prevailed, certain as he was that we can take our experiences and make them into something of beauty—art that makes meaning. Her art was teas and tinctures, perhaps the journals she wrote that contained a mixture of reflection and conversations with the herbs. Would Proust think this was art? Art helps us to get out of our own way, shift our limiting perspectives, she thought, art could cut through illusion to reveal reality, or multiple realities. When she was making a blend, when she was in the forest communing

our bodies are minerals water mud

with a hazel tree or primrose plant, it was as though she stepped beyond herself. *We think and name in one world, we live and feel in another.* In those moments she knew not only that another person did not see the universe as she saw it, but that another being, a plant being, saw landscapes that might otherwise be as distant as the moon to her, and shared something of them with her. It was in those moments that she knew which herb to choose for a particular person, asking the plants for help, her intuition not separate or the opposite of her herbal learning and experience, but available to her in ways that were hard to articulate. She had an urge to be in the forest. but late afternoon was the hottest part of the day, even in the dappled light and shade she'd soon over-heat. She hoped Émilie was home by now.

Émilie sat for a while on Deniel's favourite stump by the river, not far from the group of oaks where they had buried Viola's partner, Hugo. Others the hamlet had lost and who she and Catherine had never known, where buried beyond

the goat field, a small wooden marker with name, dates and sometimes a few words carved into each one, marking their graves. There was a similar marker for Hugo near the oaks— Hugo Benjámin Sándor, beloved—and then an odd phrase—*everything's an offer*. She had often wondered about it but felt too reticent to ask anyone, aware of her own distaste for personal questions. She had heard a lot about him, this gifted healer who seemed beloved not only by Viola but by everyone who knew him, but still the phrase was a mystery. She thought about it now after her encounter with Deniel. She'd trusted him with more of her past than anyone else from this place and was glad of it. Enough. He was someone who understood the meaning of that as well as she did. She stood and walked towards the stand of oaks, crouched by Hugo's marker and traced the letters with her fingers. Enough. She walked further into the forest where it would be cooler later, following the line of the river but higher on the bank, on the same side but out of sight of the *we make rain to cool all bodies*

hamlet. The air would be fresher in the deeper shade as the afternoon wore on. She felt a twinge of guilt for Catherine as she dropped into the long holloway at a point that would be parallel to their cottage, though across the breadth of an expanse of forest, two fields and several houses. She was in search of shade but also a vantage point. Somewhere behind the chicken runs and coops, hidden from sight, a place to watch over… She wasn't sure why, only that this is where she should be for the hours before the end. When she had found her spot she settled on a fallen beech trunk, not as comfortable as the old stump, but it would do and it wouldn't be for long. She wished she had some knitting with her. The action of her hands quieted her thoughts, took them away from those savage days in Rennes. Rose—they hadn't expected her to live. Catherine had delivered her— not that she was a midwife, but, like her, she'd grown up on a farm and was practical and, at least during the labour, brisk and confident, though once the afterbirth was taken

we make soil to nourish all bodies

care of, the cord cut and the scrap of life placed on her breast, she'd noticed how pale and shaken Catherine was. She'd felt too old to be a mother, had given up hoping for a child, but there she was, newly widowed like her friend, holed up in the apartment that had seemed so safe and comfortable less than a year ago. She remembered the estate agent showing them around the furnished flat, assuring them that the price included all bills, even Internet, and such a historic building, so close to the centre—refined and warm, were words the agent used often, and she felt impressed, awed at the prospect of living in an apartment in what had been a private mansion, 17th century, once a famous hotel and now a historical monument. She'd climbed the magnificent oak staircase wondering if this was really her life and immediately loved the flat with its huge oak beams and elegant bathroom. She'd been glad to have Catherine and Éric as neighbours when they moved to the city from

we death sensing life blossom from decay decay decay

bear

Corseul near Dinan, even happier when she discovered that Catherine was also a relative newcomer to city life. A few years older, in her mid-forties, Catherine worked at an art gallery and made her own textile pieces—hooked rugs, quilts and hand-knits. She knitted a little herself but felt reticent to say so until Catherine called one day and noticed the sweater she was working on. She found a job in a library, though her husband told her there was no need for her to work. They were secure now, could try again… She was thirty-eight and had miscarried three times already. No, she didn't think that was a good idea, and she liked to work, liked to have something to go to, people to meet… Timothée didn't press, but he was thrilled when she became unexpectedly pregnant, sure that this baby would be born safely. Like Viola's Hugo, he didn't live to meet his daughter, he and Éric dying within a couple of days of one another. Catherine moved in with her the next day, though on the surface the world was still

we life sensing death will herald new cycles

incubate

functioning. There had been pandemics before, the twenty-first century already marked by the Covid-19 and -35 pandemics, but although the numbers of deaths had seemed staggering at the time, the percentage losses of the world population remained small, less than 1%, then just under 3%. News broadcasts about the Bane mentioned figures of 30%, higher in poorer nations, though it was quickly obvious that the real numbers must be worse. What had it taken for the institutions of civilisation to unravel? Was it 20% or 50%? And in the end? The Bane burnt out more rapidly than the SARS pandemics, but its murderous work was continued by those who'd survived it. She closed her eyes as though she could shut out the images welling up. She'd learnt not to go to this place in her mind over the years, but there were days when the memories came anyway. Days like today. Enough, she whispered. Enough.

in the forest is a world and the world is life
we are your living ancestors
we are your living ancestors
we are your living ancestors

Chapter 8

She startled awake. When had she dropped off like that and for how long? Well, it was her birthday and there would be plenty of work to come. She wondered if she should make more tea or take a cold drink to Isabelle, but perhaps she was dozing too. Was Gwilherm also dozing or still poring over books? She wanted to ask him whether he'd studied psychology before, what made him interested in the subject? They had exchanged only fragments of back-story. Years ago, when she told him that she came from Ireland he'd continued the conversation in good English. His mother had taught him. She knew that his mother had been Hungarian and an artist, Flóra, but nothing more about his family. She wandered across to the window—everything as before—ready and waiting. She was no good at this— waiting, relaxing. No-one needed her to fetch them drinks, Lisette was with her friends, clearly plotting some surprise.

we are the ground of your being
we are the ground of your being
we are the ground of your being
in the earth are words and the words are health
we are the ground of your being

103

in the forest is a world and the world is life
your ancestors evolved in forest
ancestors evolved in forest
evolved in forest
in forest

She sat at the little desk that had been Hugo's and opened
the drawer. She would use the originals today—a double
birthday, the Summer Solstice, worrying about what she
should do next for Deniel, wondering if the future might
hold… how should she phrase her question? There was no
point asking the cards something so wide that the answer
would be a meaningless blur. She wished Hugo was there to
help her interpret. What would he think of her life now,
of… She shook herself. She would show the cards to Isabelle
later, get another perspective. She held the pack in her hand.
She had not known her grandfather but he'd felt so alive in
the stories Saoirse told, Oisín Ó Murcháin, son of Daireann,
a woman who became legendary around Reagh—tiny, wiry,
with cropped hair and eyes so dark they were almost black.
And an affinity with a huge male hare that frequented her
fields. Her card readings had been powerful gifts. She
reached into the drawer and took out a string of beads,
amethyst, fluorite, moonstone, red jasper and tiger eye that

in the earth are words and the words are health
your ancestors were nourished by the forest
ancestors were nourished by the forest
were nourished by the forest
by the forest

104

first walked upright
branches you first walked upright
in our branches you first walked upright
in the forest is a world and the world is life

had belonged to Daireann. Saoirse had insisted that she take it when she left Reagh to travel to Berrien. She felt the cool weight of the stones in her hands then slipped them over her head, hoping her great-grandmother would give her insight. She shuffled the cards and focussed on her question, laying out a world tree spread, turning each card slowly—three of pentacles, the root of the issue. Oisín had painted a couple, a knight and a woman in simple peasant dress with a falcon flying between them, taking his inspiration from the story of Érec and Énide. Érec had pursued a knight who had insulted Gwenhwyfar and, when he finally caught up with him, he met Énide, the daughter of a poor tenant farmer, and fell in love. He entered a tournament to win a falcon for the most beautiful woman there. Having defeated the insulting knight, won the falcon and presented it to Énide, he married her and returned to Arthur's court. But Érec's comrades felt that he ignored his duties in favour of staying close to his bride and when she heard about this, she became

you homes
gave you homes
rootedness gave you homes
our rootedness gave you homes
in the earth are words and the words are health

105

in the forest   we sheltered
          is a world   your ancestors
thousands   and the world
          of seasons ago   is life

so distressed that Érec told her to prepare for travel and they set out to defend his honour. Along the way, Énide regularly saved Érec's life with her sharp eye for danger. And so they became the epitome of co-operative work, going on to become the King and Queen of Nantes, their falcon always beside them. This was the root of her answer, then, not going it alone. Of course, she didn't, she consulted Isabelle and Lisette all the time, but that wasn't what she had asked about… this would be a wholly different type of… what? Collaboration? Relationship? There was a knock on her door and she covered the spread on her desk with a scarf draped on the back of the chair, wondering why she done that…

Gwilherm opened the door but stayed on the threshold. Come in, she welcomed, smiling, I was getting restless with my own company. Really? His surprise was genuine, she always seemed so self-contained, even when… and he'd heard Lisette teasing her about how she had a gift for being oblivious to everything going on around her when she was

in the earth   for millions
          are words   of moons
we have healed   and the words
          your ancestors   are health

our story is your story is our story is your

in the forest is a world and the world is life

your story is our story is your story is our

focussed on something—reading, cooking, journalling, blending herbs… She laughed. Trapped time, she said. If I've got something I want to be doing I can go for hours, days, probably weeks on my own, but give me a liminal bit of trapped time and I'm like a caged wolf. He nodded, filing away the information. Well if you're feeling at a loose end, I was wondering if you'd thought any more about… I have, she said, or at least I am. She pulled the scarf from the desk and he moved towards the cards she'd laid out there. They're beautiful. Do you know who the artist was? She showed him the box lid, painted in gold lettering: The Brocéliande Tarot, Oisín Ó Murcháin. My grandfather painted them when he and Sarah, my grandmother, were living near Paimpont and my mother was a child. It's where they met Isabelle, she was there when he died, a heart condition that no-one knew about. He traced the outline of the figure on the card at the top of the spread—the magician. Merlin? he asked. Yes, Myrddin Emrys, or Myrddin Wyllt, perhaps one and the

your story is our story is your story is our story

in the earth are words and the words are health

our story is your story is our story is your story

same, but also a self portrait of Oisín. It's one I particularly love. Can I show you my other favourites? she asked, reaching for the heel of the deck. I'd love to see them. She sat on the edge of the bed and he sat too, making space between them for her to place cards. This is the Hermit— my great grandmother Daireann. She'd travelled and learnt Chinese herbalism as well as using local herbs. The hare was her familiar. She's wearing the necklace you have on, he said. Viola fingered the string of beads. Yes, it belonged to her and then to my mother, she gave it to me when I left Reagh. She took a deep breath. This is the High Priestess—painted as Viviane, Merlin's apprentice and love. May I? She nodded and he picked up the image of a beautiful woman dressed in a simple cobalt-blue tunic and rising from a turquoise blue lake, a white-gold crystal haze shimmering around from her as the waters parted, the day clear yet with a single star blazing in the background of hot blue sky. In her arms she carried the bough of an apple tree sprouting two apples, one gold, one red. She looks like the woman Lisette will become, he said. Yes. It's actually Sarah, my grandmother, but my mother and Lisette look exactly like her. I look like my dad—she laid the King of Pentacles on the bed—a wolf surveying his territory, a landscape in full bloom, lush trees, bright flowers and a full moon rising even though it was day time. Your dad was a wolf? She laughed. His name meant 'wolf', Faolán. In the Fianna, Faolán is the one who would rescue Fionn mac Cumhaill from God himself. He rescued my mother once. She placed the Lovers next to the wolf card—this is what he looked like—Oisín used the story of Tristrem and Ysonde for the Forest Lovers, but the models are Faolán and Saoirse. He looked up, puzzled, But surely your grandfather could never have met your father? She picked up the card. Not in this world, she said softly, then gazed at him directly so that he wondered if this was a test. Was she gauging his reaction? Are there others he knew beyond his life? He hoped he sounded like he trusted her

in the forest is a world and the world is life
in our branches you first walked upright

story, strange as it was. Yes—this one—my favourite of all favourites. She placed the Hierophant card down, a teacher and mentor, a wise ancestor who interprets the sacred mysteries. Oisín had painted him not as a priest but a young man seated in a lotus position beneath a huge hazel tree, holding a key that ended in a pentangle. He had light brown hair that curled and knotted, hazel eyes. He wore a blue tunic over fawn yoga trousers. In the background, a stag watched him. This is Hugo, she said, her voice catching. He wanted to reach out to her, but hesitated a moment too long, cursing himself. Ah, and my mother's individual card—the girl in the image is Saoirse aged around ten. He noticed she too had Lisette's wild dark hair, caught in a loose band at her neck. She was about to dive into a river from which a salmon leapt further upstream. In many tarots the Fool is accompanied by a small dog, Viola told him, but in Oisín's there's this wild cat, perhaps a mountain lion. And this, her voice was bright again, is me—the card of the

in the earth are words and the words are health
our rootedness gave you homes

Queen of Cups was Viola in the forest, a crescent moon hanging in a dusk sky. An owl flew from a stand of oaks and in the turbulent river in the foreground, another salmon leapt upstream. The image of Viola was crouched between woodland and river, harvesting a violet plant, in her hand she held the steel sickle he had given her earlier that day. He heard his breath as though it was filling the room and she put a hand on his arm. We're a lot to fathom, the tribes of Jacobs and Ó Murcháins and Sándors. He wanted to say the right thing, but all that came out was, And the MacAonghusas? My father always maintained he was very ordinary, just loyal and in love. He smiled. I like him, I mean I would have liked to have known him. There was a silence and he watched Viola begin to look through the cards again, then put them down. But enough for now, she said, I've completely diverted you from what you came to ask me and all I can say is I'm thinking…

in the forest are worlds within worlds
listen, wolves upon a time before…
see in the moss the woodwife stirs
feel the breath of the ancient oak

Chapter 9

She sat down again at her desk, it would not be long now till people began arriving back. Alain was already there, putting the finishing touches to the gather-hall, and Gwilherm had gone to help him. She wondered if their conversation might turn to discussing her and laughed at herself. She would go and finish the reading—she had the roots of collaboration from the three of pentacles, the wonderful possibilities of the magician as the branches of her tree spread. What else was there to find? In her room she lifted the next card—the position of the east—what she would take with her on the the next part of her journey—the page of pentacles was an androgynous figure standing on the brow of a hill surveying the land ahead, the earth fertile, a settlement in the distance under a Summer sky. The page's feet were firmly planted and around them dandelions and burdock grew, herbs with strong and nourishing roots, herbs that helped to root those

feel the ancient earth reach within you
see in tree-trunks portals to the otherworld
listen, spirits upon a time before…
in the forest are worlds within worlds

in the mirror of lake is the fée Morgane
in the cave Korrigan sirens her dreams
in the rocks l'homme vert beckons the birds
in the chaos bones rest under the earth

who ate them. Wood betony purpled the slope of the hill—known as a panacea for centuries, it was another deeply grounding herb. Stability, security—these would not be left behind. But to the west was the Hanged Man—not caught in a noose or bound, but hanging like a child daring to swing from a branch by his legs, a card for breaking old patterns, letting go, sometimes a card concerned with sacrifice and loss. To leave loss and sacrifice behind, what might that mean? She thought about her relationship with Alain—it had always been doomed, but perhaps it would have been less painful for both of them if she had been less sacrificing, less unwilling to name her boundaries. Even with Hugo she had swallowed feelings rather than challenge, though he'd had a knack for rejecting her sacrifices. She did the same with her daughter, with those she was treating—over-working, tempted to help beyond what was helpful. If she let go of that? She turned to the card of the south, her hopes—the knight of cups—creativity, beauty, romance,

invisible you cross the universe in a moment
rise without wings go through the ground
enter everywhere closed windows doors
and decide when to let yourself be seen

enmesh the heart
    enchant the soul
        enliven dreams
            entrap the disloyal

exciting news… a card that told her to follow her heart, and yet the card to the north, her fears, was the knight of wands—full of energy, passion and inspiration, a card that said things would get better than she realised, that she should take action, had a chance to make a change for the good. Why would this be a fear? And yet she felt its truth— the two knight cards mirroring each other—her hopes and fears were entwined, what she wanted was also what made her anxious. Which would win? The card for the way back through the forest suggested the victory of hope over fear, the ace of cups brimming with love, compassion, creative spirit, a new awakening. The picture was of one of the ancient stone washing basins shaped like a large cist that were found around rivers throughout Brittany. Water flowed into it from a river and a deer had stopped to drink there. And the final card—the wisdom of the world tree, was the ten of cups, a promise of love, the reassurance that everything needful was already there in abundance. The

round Keramperluven's stone Korrigans dance
    nocturnal frenetic wild they spin and howl
        while polpegan shape-shift among leaves
            and red lulius appear as horses to ride.

to taste the sweet aril of the yew without bitter seed
to breathe the linden when it is a volcano of bees
to hear the branches murmur stories to stars
to touch the depths of the magical pool

image was of the small waterfall that tumbled over the chaos of Ice Age boulders in the river below L'Autre Rive, a place Oisín had never visited. By the side of the river a woman was filling ten vessels with the clear, pure water. Some were earthenware, with the marks that Christophe used on his pots, one was a a big copper pan that hung in L'Autre Rive's kitchen, another a large orange pot, stove-scorched but beautiful, and also from her kitchen. The woman filling the pots was slender and elegant with pale golden hair, beautiful, like spun silk, and the palest blue eyes—Isabelle, as Oisín had known her, in her early thirties, but in the forest of Huelgoat. It was a powerful card to represent the wisdom of the world tree, she thought, communicating deep contentment, a sense of being safe and in the right place, surrounded by beauty. And she was, even in such a crazy world, she was privileged to live in this place, with these people, to be able to work with the healing plants, to be able to accompany Deniel on the last stages of his journey

here you walk in the wood from above
here amongst roots Merlin lies entombed
here among boulders Rome Arthur made camp
here walked Jean and Jeanette to the devil's cottage

here walked Jean and Jeanette to the devil's cottage
here among boulders Roue Arzhur made camp
here amongst roots Merzhin lies entombed
here you walk in the wood from above

and now to have... She heard the sound of voices, neighbours arriving to begin the feast. Good. Tomorrow she would talk through the cards with Isabelle, but for now there was celebrating to be done. She looked down at the garden, people arriving with more food, Gwilherm and Zoé tuning violins, Isabelle, radiant in the blue silk scarf that rippled like water, greeting people, and Lisette handing out drinks, the hostess at ease.

Lisette handed a glass to Julie and another to Pascal. She noticed a tiny ripple of movement across Julie's belly and had an urge to ask if she could feel the baby. Julie smiled. She's moving all the time now, she said. She? Julie put a hand on the bump, It's just a feeling, maybe because the pregnancy seems different to the one with Pascal, easier this time. Lisette nodded. She thought she'd talk to Carène soon, ask if she would train her as a midwife. It would go well with herbalism, and she was fascinated by new life, helping it into the world, being part of what would come next. She looked

to taste the sweet air of the yew without bitter seed
to breathe the linden when it is a volcano of bees
to heal the branches minimum stolies to slays
to touch the depths of the magical pool

round Kérampeulven's stone korrigans dance
  nocturnal frenetic wild they spin and howl
      while polpegan shape-shift among leaves
          and red lutins appear as horses to ride

up. Viola was standing at her bedroom window and they both waved. She hoped Viola had rested, hadn't run around finding more to do than was needed. There was a difference in her this last couple of weeks, an interiority that she sensed was more than Viola's usual penchant for oblivion, something new. She'd mentioned it to Isabelle who had only smiled and raised her palms to the heavens in that way she had when she knew more than she was prepared to say. Alice arrived with her family, flushed and carrying her flute in a case over her shoulder and balancing a tray of food. Well, at least I only have one mother to worry about, she thought, then immediately thought of Isabelle, though it had never felt the same as with Viola—she had been something between grandchild and apprentice to Isabelle for as long as she could remember, though Isabelle never played the role of mother with Viola, they were sisters in herbs, separated by a mere fifty-three years. Are you nervous? Alice asked when she'd deposited her tray of food on the long table

enmesh the heart
enchant the soul
enliven dreams
enrapt the disloyal

117

invisible you cross the universe in a moment
rise without wings go through the ground
enter everywhere closed windows doors
and decide when to let yourself be seen

under the awning that ran along the side of the house. She paused to consider. I don't think I am. I was this morning when I woke, but once we'd rehearsed the last time, it felt right—the right gift. It doesn't have to be perfect, just… given, I suppose. And I couldn't do it without you and Zoé. Alice coloured and grinned. That makes me feel better, she said. And Zoé looks relaxed. She and Gwilherm had tuned up and were trying out some dance melodies on the arrivals. He's good, isn't he? She studied the duo—Very good, she agreed. I'll be back in a moment, there's something I want to check. Alice turned to her friend, Are you okay? You look… a bit… pale, well a bit green actually. She tried to smile, should she tell Alice what she had just noticed? She wanted to, but it felt too… too what? I'm fine, just a small thing I forgot. She disappeared into the building and made for the desk at the back of the L-shaped bend of their downstairs room. The desk stood by the back window with an old sofa and chairs ranged around the rest of the space.

in the mirror of lake is the fée Morgane
in the cave Korrigan silence her dreams
in the rocks I humming very beckons the birds
in the chaos bounce rest under the earth

in the forest are worlds within worlds
　　　listen, spirits upon a time before…
　　　　　see in tree-trunks portals to the otherworld
　　　　　　　feel the ancient earth reach within you

She opened the central drawer and took out the copy of the Brocéliande Tarot that had been the given to Isabelle the day her great-grandfather died, passing through other hands to come to her father and then back to Isabelle. She wanted to race through the pack but the injunction to handle the well-used cards with care was deeply ingrained. It was almost the last card she came to—there he was— the king of cups, a figure of emotional balance, compassion and diplomacy. She had seen the card so many times, perhaps thousands—in the foreground the river that ran beneath L'Autre Rive, a heron standing in the water where it pooled after flowing over the boulders, poised and waiting with infinite patience for the prize to come to him. And on the river bank, the knight, Bedivere, the loyal cup-bearer, and yes… she was right, there he was…

feel the breath of the ancient oak
see in the moss the woodwife stirs
listen, woives upon a time before…
in the forest are worlds within worlds

as below, above
root-like we stretch into sky,
kiss the rising sun.

Chapter 10

She still had the song in her head, the melody so simple, so beautiful. She looked around. Lisette was deep in conversation with Isabelle, both of them animated and happy. Gwilherm had fetched his violin from the vardo and he and Zoé were beginning a dance tune, Pierrick picking up his guitar to join them. Whatever the future held, this was a good day. She had thought she might stop breathing when she lost Hugo, but here she was, among friends, brimming with love for her daughter, his daughter, grateful for life. Deniel was moving around the group, friends embracing him, back patting, exchanging the bise. He must be taking his leave early. He'd watched the children's entertainment, heard the girls' birthday song, spent time with neighbours and family, though only picking at food, she'd noted earlier. He stopped to talk to Gwilherm before coming towards her and held out his arms, Happy birthday,

buried
our roots shelter the patience
of the faithful earth

we are not baubles
prettying a drab landscape,
but life breathing life

Viola. And thank you. Thank you for everything. She hugged him tightly, feeling how his weight was lightening each week, perhaps even more rapidly. Thank you for all you've done for me. She studied him for a moment. It's the herbs that do the real work, she replied, but thank you for listening to them. There were tears in his eyes. Well, I'm grateful to you and the herbs. I'm grateful for more than I can say. He gestured towards the gathering. For all of it. But right now, I need to sleep. A good, long sleep. He smiled and she nodded. Would you like me to walk with you? He shook his head. I'm fine and you should be here. She watched his slow walk until he disappeared around the far side of the noisy girls' house. You're deep in thought. Lisette was beside her, flushed and smiling. I just said good night to Deniel, she said. She shivered. You look pale, Lisette said. Oh, I'm fine, just worrying about him. We all do, Lisette replied. He knows you're doing everything you can and... She hugged her daughter. Look at me, surrounded by friends and getting

in the silent depths
geology, bodies,   all
decay beneath us

still woman vigils,
we will keep this watch with her,
hold her till it's done

melancholy. Lisette smiled. I think it's okay to be happy and sad at the same time—they're not opposites at all. She hugged Lisette again. You're right. And Deniel has had a good evening. All we need now is for Émilie to appear. Stop worrying, Lisette told her, laughing. Anyway, Isabelle read Catherine's tarot just now and she's absolutely sure Émilie's okay.

Émilie had sat through much of the afternoon in the forest on the old fallen beech trunk She'd heard the gong at L'Autre Rive banging to signal that people should go home and rest for the afternoon and saw Gaëlle-Anne returning home with the boys. So they would be with Deniel for a few hours, though Alex must have stayed behind to tend to the slow roasting boar. Yes—there he was, returning perhaps an hour or more later. All at home. Still she sat and watched, aware of the rising humidity in the air, even under the shade of the beech trees, hotter than she liked but not unbearable. She wished again that her hands were occupied, worried

in the heart beat's   space
                    between silence   and breathing
life dies
           becomes life

122

we suspend your view,
curve your perspective, foretell
of new horizons.

about Catherine, tried to think of things that would keep the past at bay. Later in the afternoon, Alex left the longère ahead of the others, returning to his roasting duties and carrying a large pot of something to add to the feast, something that would be delicious, though she could not imagine wanting to eat today. Gaëlle-Anne and the children left a while later, the twins carrying hessian sacks, no doubt stuffed with sourdough loaves, and their mother carrying a large flat dish. She eased herself into another position on the fallen trunk and waited. Soon, Deniel walked in the direction of the feast. She smiled. Of course he would want it to go well. Even now he must be thinking… But no, it was useless to guess at another person's private thoughts. She tracked him at a distance, keeping below the line of sight in the cooling holloway. She could hear the babble of people setting up the food, the sound of children, excited and happy, not yet over-tired, laughter and a bubble of song that rose on the air. Aimée, she thought—she sang constantly, as

roots excavate
dive   e a r t h
    through bottomless humus,
seek out hidden   light

petals of the heart
astringe the day, soften night,
ah, such fragrant love

though unaware she was doing so—and another voice—confident, pitch-perfect—Véronique, who taught the children alongside her brother. Alain was charismatic—a gifted story-teller, an astute observer and a talented visual artist, his sister calm and organised, musical but also analytical, able to teach the children maths and logic. Nearly everyone in the village taught in different ways—passing on crafts and skills, Sébastien communicating his love of sciences, Carène teaching anatomy and talking to the older children about sexuality and gender, the beekeepers sharing their secrets, Viola instilling her love of plants so deeply that all of them, adults and children alike, had their particular familiars among these other beings. Rose. She and Viola shared this passion—Viola was also named for rose—Viola Róisin, yet she had never told Viola why rose was her companion plant. She'd sensed that she didn't have to—Viola had the knack of knowing what was needed even when it wasn't obvious to anyone else, of divining without

strong wood bur$_{row}$$_{ing}$
thin roots f$_{an}$$_{n}$$_i$n^g out for food

together we stand

124

upwards, we silver,
birch-straight, make invisible
the lost distances.

asking intrusive questions. A gong sounded and she edged closer to the gathering, still being careful to stay out of sight. People finished loading food onto plates, filled their glasses and began to take seats around the garden tables. She scanned the group. Catherine was seated at one of the larger tables. Alice brought her a plate of food and a glass and returned to the long table at the side of the building to get something for herself, returning with her family. She saw Zélie reach out a hand and squeeze Catherine's arm briefly, Sébastien and Francine nodding at something Zélie had said in that moment of reassurance. She sighed. She had no wish to make her dearest friend anxious. Soon Catherine would understand, she told herself. Joceline stopped beside her family's table and gestured towards a little stage that had been erected in front of the small barn that Viola used as her pharmacy, then headed off to join her friends. A group of younger children were already assembled around the platform, excited, Pascal and Armel jigging from foot to

. downwards we tunnel
intersect and cross
bury us
grounding through aeons

125

cells beneath bark skin,
sapwood under growing cells.
dead heartwood holds life.

foot. Alain stood on the stage and gestured for quiet, then beckoned forward a small group. The children's performances began with tunes on wooden recorders that were greeted with rapturous applause, then there was a mini-play about a greedy elf, Ronan in the starring role. Afterwards, André, Gigi and Joceline sang a clutch of Breton folk songs, Pierrick accompanying them on guitar. He'd had an angelic voice until recently, but it was breaking and would emerge as another voice soon. Thank you, friends, Véronique said, her voice carrying to the edge of the wood. When the clapping subsided she went on. We'll have a fifteen minute break and then we have a very special performance after the interval. More applause and people stretching and chatting, queuing for the roast or for the noisy girls' succulent chicken. The scents wafted towards her, but still she had no appetite. Deniel was with his grandsons, each competing for attention as he helped them to food and smiled at everything they said. She felt a pang

transparent roundworms;
noodle-shaped, moist rotifers—
          h   i
       hair-crowns   —feed

126

rings embody all—
famine and glut, fire and drought,
what bends and shapes us.

of loneliness wash over her, so drenching that she wondered
about joining the others, but if she did so now how would
she be able to escape when the time… She'd steadied her
breath. Soon. The musicians after the intermission were
Lisette, Zoé and Alice. Lisette introduced the piece, she'd
written it for her mother's fortieth birthday and there was a
pause while Viola stood and toasted her daughter and
everyone cheered, raised glasses and applauded. Whatever
their strains and struggles, conflicts or memories stirred by
this day, for this evening the spirit of birthdays and
midsummer would prevail. The audience settled and the
song began, Lisette's voice supple and bright, but with an
undertone, a depth that surprised her from a teenager, even
one as assured as Lisette appeared to be. She felt soothed and
moved at once, but not only by the voice, the delicacy of
Alice's flute was like the clearest river on the hottest day and
Zoé's violin was the depth's of the water's flow—mineral-
rich, full of life. She realised she was crying, not sobs, but a

    roots   like fingers   trace
d d   to the beginning
o o   of rock,   soil,   knowledge
w w
n n

127

we tremble in wind,
seed particles to make rain,
panic as it falls.

stream of joy and sorrow more cathartic than all the howling
she'd done years ago. Such a gift—for Viola, for all of them.
She scanned those she could see from her cloistered vantage
point, more than one hand brushing away a tear, the same
faces smiling, transported. Catherine was turned away from
her, but her shoulders rocked a little and, either side of her,
Zélie and Francine rested a hand lightly on shoulder and
arm. When the piece ended she felt bereft for a moment,
then lighter than she had felt in... ever? There was silence in
the garden, a wave of collective in-breath, then they stood,
cries of brava, cheers, a sea of applause. The girls stood
completely still for a second then fell into an embrace,
fanned out and bowed, hugged again before the crowd
descended on them, clasping them, congratulating, asking a
hundred questions. She noticed Viola watching it all, letting
the hubbub subside, then moving to take Lisette in her
arms, both of them weeping and laughing, Isabelle joining
them and Viola hugging Alice and Zoé in turn. She watched

we make our way round
granite,t r e m b l e when earth burns,
swell with Winter rain,

sweet tang of almond
above camphor, wintergreen,
healing's bitter note.

her community. Even Catherine looked less burdened, she thought. Every year they celebrated this feast, every year Isabelle and Viola's birthdays fell on this day, three years ago Isabelle's ninetieth birthday had been a hootenanny of a day, but surely there would never be another like this. She waited at her post, watching more of the entertainment, the mingling in between, the boar getting smaller... At last Deniel began moving among his neighbours, clasping them to him, kissing cheeks, nodding. Ronan and Paol alongside him. He bent at last and said something to them, put a hand on each head, then squatted and hugged each of them, the effort of the movement obviously painful, even viewed from a distance. He paused longer with Viola before he set off towards his longère. She walked on the top path of the forest, the banks lush with fern and meadowsweet, the plants alive with butterflies and moths, emerging onto the lane just past the smokehouse, out of sight of L'Autre Rive's garden, hidden from Deniel by the barns and the solid

fibres   en
     twining
mud   clinging to
       8   h   hairs
           g   sucking nourishment

Breton house where Claire lived with Brigitte and Diane. He stopped when he drew alongside his home, turning to face it, bowing slightly, then walked on. She edged around the beekeeper's barn as he disappeared around the farthest buildings of the hamlet—a cluster of small cottages that were uninhabited, but the furthest two, still maintained, attached cottages each with one room upstairs and one down plus a tiny bathroom at the back. The community had agreed that they should have somewhere for emergencies—someone with an illness that seemed to pose a threat to them all, someone from outside seeking refuge… Or one of their own, like Deniel, seeking another type of sanctuary.

Deniel had walked slowly towards his home. Earlier, he'd left notes—for Alex, Gaëlle-Anne, another for the boys, for Viola and one for the community. He'd planned them over and over as he walked Fragan each day, sat on the stump in the forest, but had left the writing to today, anxious that they should not be inadvertently found too early. He'd

below, amoebas
life—shape-shifting to slime moulds
ooze within the earth

you can see the wood,
for the trees, each one of us
witness to the whole.

begun gathering and drying yew needles and seeds last Autumn, savouring the fleshy arils of the berries, so light and sweet, the only non-toxic part of the tree. He'd considered many ways of doing this, but most were too gruesome for others to find or had a high risk of failure. He had no desire to suffer and hoped that taking as high a dose as possible would at least make him lose consciousness more quickly. He stopped not far from his longère and turned towards it. Thank you, he said into the warm evening air and bowed towards the home that had given him more than he could recount if he lived another seventy-two years. He paused, wondering if someone was watching him. Shook himself. No, there was no-one around. He walked on towards the empty cottages and let himself in to the farthest small house. He'd thought about visiting earlier to light the small wood stove so that he could heat water more quickly but it would have made it stifling inside and, even on the edge of the hamlet, there was the chance of someone

tardigrades—eight-leg-
ged gummy bears with claws and
spiky mouths—suction

noticing the smoke. He'd have to take that chance now but the cottage was well out of view of L'Autre Rive. It must be around seven o'clock and the festivities would go on into the early hours of the morning. There would be story telling in the gather-hall, and later, around the fire pit, the community ceremony of Alban Hefin to complement the private hopes, wishes, perhaps even prayers, that some of them might have spoken that morning. If he was lucky his own ritual might be over before midnight. If it took longer, Alex and Gaëlle-Anne would assume he was asleep when they wandered home, tired, most likely leaving the boys to sleep on a mattress at L'Autre Rive as they had done last year. They'd sleep late unless Fragan woke them, disturbed by his change in routine, impatient for his early walk. He shook his head. The thought of their worry, their loss… but it was coming whatever he did and this way they would not have to endure the long last weeks of caring for someone who could not breathe properly, perhaps could not take in food,

in a thrill of wind
leaves pray to infinite light,
knowing dark will come.

or even liquids, whose pain was beyond control. He'd tried
to say a little of this in the notes, but he hadn't wanted to
dwell too much on it—more than anything he wanted to
leave gratitude behind. He laid kindling in the stove and
began coaxing the fire into life, setting a large kettle on top.
He fetched the seeds and needles from a tin in the tiny loft
space, adding them to the water in the kettle. Upstairs in the
little bedroom, the old iron bed was neatly made. He'd taken
a length plastic from one of the rolls stored in a barn to lay
under the bottom sheet in case of vomiting or diarrhoea,
though an irrational part of him hoped he wouldn't be
found in such a mess. He smiled, even in death he wanted
to be seen as calm and clean. He thought back over the day.
It had been good—from his morning walk with Fragan to
that exquisite and haunting song that Lisette had written for
Viola, wonderful moments with Ronan and Paol and that
small and moving encounter with Émilie, an unexpected
gift. He hoped she was okay. He hadn't realised that people

in the turned webs
earth worships the gentle dark,
knowing its comfort

we take the long view,
immortal, we bring you death,
understand healing.

were worried about Émilie until he returned to the party but had reassured Catherine that Émilie had simply gone for a walk after setting the tables and Isabelle set her mind at rest with a tarot reading. The kettle began to sing softly and he lifted it onto a thin trivet for the tea to decoct, ten minutes later carrying the pot upstairs together with the large mug he'd brought from home the previous day. It was one that Christophe had made, a pale biscuit colour with a rounded body that sat well in the hand, given as a gift from his family. He looked around the room, calm and ready. He walked over to the small window and scanned the village, again that sense of being watched, surely nothing more than his anxiety that he might be disturbed, or was there a shadow by the corner of the uninhabited house close to the cottages? The sun was getting a little lower, though it would be hours before it set completely, a trick of the light, but a niggle remained. Had Émilie gone back to the gathering? Surely by now…

roots *toxic as bark,*
toxic as berries, as leaves,

darkest remedy

134

branches bathe in light
sky suckles leaves until sun
bows to promised night

Émilie stood by the abandoned house. She realised she'd been holding her breath, watching Deniel at the cottage window. He moved into the room and she crouched against the wall of the decaying building. How long should she wait?

roots feast on the soil,
minerals nurture each cell,
long rhythm of thanks.

buds, flowers and leaves
in the clear Solstice light
Summer's brief promise.

Chapter 11

She stood at the back of the gather-hall. The children were
ranged around Alain. Pascal, Armel and the twins cross-
legged at the front, Gigi, Joceline, André and Pierrick,
behind them, Pierrick, who'd recently had a growth spurt,
looking uneasy in the group. André, a year younger, still at
ease, laughing at something his sister, Gigi, had just said.
Lisette, Zoé and Alice had not joined the little huddle close
to the story tellers, but sat on cushions scattered amongst
the chairs where the adults seated themselves as they drifted
in ready for the performances. Some brought in plates, most
a glass. A ring of candles around the stage area added
atmosphere, but the real lighting came from their still-
functioning EverLights, descendants of a project started
early in the twenty-first century to bring lighting without
batteries or electricity to communities in Africa, who'd still
been reliant on expensive and dangerous kerosene lamps.

wood rot, microbes, worms,
dead leaves, humus, warming mulch
Summer's rich blessings.

feel our boundaries—
needles of folic acid,
sharp sting of healing,

The first lamps used gravity with weights and pulleys and later a mixture of solar and gravity-powered mini generators that hooked to a daisy chain of lights. They'd become ubiquitous in the thirties, popular for lighting barns, for camping trips or to use during increasingly frequent power cuts. Since the Shift, the LEDs in the oldest ones had died, but many were still working well and some would last another ten years, perhaps fifteen with careful use. The last fourteen years, since the Shift settled into the way things were now, had been hard, but what would future years be like for these children sitting waiting for the story to begin? For Lisette? They had little that could pass for technology. The EverLights in the gather-hall had been brought from all the houses in the hamlet. Most had at least a couple, some three or four, as well as the daisy-chained SaterLights. Gwilherm had foraged a micro-hydro-generator from an empty mill house but they used it only for keeping the meat-preparation barn cold, relying on the root cellars for

root within to clean
and clear, flush out irritants,
cool, calm and protect.

high Summer's woodwose,
tannin-rich, masting acorns
for the sweet green earth.

other cool stores, or on evaporation boxes and zeer pots for what they kept indoors, particularly from Spring to Autumn. They wouldn't be able to fix the generator when it finally went, or replace the EverLights when their LEDs no longer shone. Slowly, they were heading for a deeper Dark Age unless there were changes in the wider world that they knew nothing of. No such news came back with Gwilherm as he roamed his small territory, swapping items with other foragers, nor from the occasional travellers who passed by. Did Lisette think similar thoughts, wonder how she would live in this precarious world, how she might meet a future partner or raise children herself? She hadn't had to think of such things when she was fifteen, blissfully oblivious to what was coming, living with Sarah, Saoirse and Faolán in a remote part of Roscommon—remote, but never cut off. Friends came to stay, the Internet proliferated, phones linked them every hour of the day, VirRea sites offered meet-ups advertised as indistinguishable from the 'real

and beneath our roots
flesh and leaf mulch and compost,
nurturing new life.

wound healing leaves, soft-
cushion pain, soothe into sleep,
whispering *relax*.

thing', though her family remained firmly Luddite in that respect. At least these children and young people had no memories of the all-pervasiveness of technology. Would that make their lives easier to navigate? Mes amis, if I can have your attention, please. A hush fell and people settled into silence, all attention on Alain. Our story this evening has been richly illustrated by a group of artists of incomparable skill. Artists, if you will take a bow. The two rows of children stood, grinning, Pierrick shepherding the smaller ones to change places with the second row so that they could be at the front to face the audience. On three, Pierrick said, counting quietly. Pascal waved wildly to Julie and Noé as the others made exaggerated bows and the adults applauded and cheered. While the children took their seated places again, Alain signalled to Hervé to pull the cord of a light behind a white bedsheet that hung across the makeshift stage. The shadows of flowers and owls bloomed on the fabric. The feathers of the owls looking like leaves and petals, the

roots to root out harm,
to clear away blockages—
essence of solace

sex and life and death,
here is green fertility—
the world in a seed,

flowers sometimes resembling the beak or eye of an owl. The audience breathed in as one, already under Alain's spell. She loved the story of Blodeuwedd, the name meaning both 'flower face' and 'owl', made for a man cursed by his mother, Arianrhod, who had been deceived into conceiving a child by her brother, Gwydion, a powerful magician who wanted his son to be king, but knew the line would pass through his sister. To thwart Gwydion, Arianrhod cursed her child to have no name, no right to bear arms and never to marry a human woman. Gwydion and his uncle, Math, overcame the first two curses, but the third was harder and so they created a woman from nine magical flowers—nettle and oak, primrose, bean, broom, meadowsweet, burdock, chestnut and hawthorn. She was the tarot's Empress, the green goddess, the earth in bloom, the sovereignty of the land, Alain pronounced, the tale in full flow. Married to her, Llew could rule. But who can take the sovereignty of the land against her will? What happens when men think that

bitter digestive,
tonic for appetite, skin,
and, ah, fevers cooled.

when swelling eases
and vessel walls grow stronger,
blood returns to heart

the earth is theirs for the bidding? They were living the answer to that, she thought, looking around at the rapt faces. But the spirit of the land will not be so easily owned, Alain went on, and so the day came when Llew was away from home and Blodeuwedd met another man. Gronw was his name, a huntsman of more skill than our own Gilles, perhaps even more stealthy than Cloé, and as handsome as Hervé. The crowd cheered and Hervé made a bow from the side of the stage. But what could they do? Llew would never let her go until he died. And so Blodeuwedd and Gronw plotted to kill him. But how? When Blodeuwedd pretended to be fearful for Llew's safety he told her not to worry, he was protected by Math and Gwydion, whose magic ensured he could not could not be killed either outdoors or in, not on horse nor on foot, and only with a spearhead cast during a sacred period of time. She discussed the problem with Gronw and they came up with a plan. He would spend a year making the spearhead, the period of sacred time, and

cramp ease, itching gone,
softening of arteries,
softening within.

sweet for digestion
green scent salving every pain,
how soft dissolves stones.

afterwards she would ask Llew to show her how difficult it would be to kill him. And he did. He prepared a bath at the side of the river, had a thatched roof erected over it and stood in the bathwater—see, neither inside nor out… He clambered onto the edge of the bath, then reached one foot out of the bath and rested it onto the back of a goat, waiting in position. See, neither on horse nor on foot. And as he was speaking Gronw's arrow was flying towards him and lodged in his side. Dead! Alain's voice rang out and it wasn't only the children nearest him who jumped. Dead, he said more quietly, or was he? The slumped body rose, not an injured man but an eagle, bleeding but capable of flight—rose and rose and was gone. But not for long. Math and Gwydion searched for Llew and treated his wounds, bringing him back to his human form. And then they searched for the lovers and when they found them Gronw was killed, but Blodeuwedd they transformed into an owl, a bird of night and death. And still to this day in the land where

red-brown rhizome creeps
through shaded loam, rich and moist,
sweet roots to console.

142

Blodeuwedd was made, her name means both flower face and owl. She watched Alain pause for the barest moment before taking his own bow. She wanted to be flowers, but not owned, she thought. She watched Alain colouring to the applause, happy with his day's work, with Hervé close by. She and Alain had not been happy in their brief time together as a couple, though Lisette had adored him. There were days when she hadn't known whether she was flowers or owl. She had wanted to be flowers—the healing of oak and nettle, primrose, bean, broom, meadowsweet, burdock, chestnut and hawthorn. But there was something in Alain she could never reach, something that did not need healing, only acknowledging. Her own path was impossible to walk while she tried to live for Alain, and he for her. There had been no betrayal between them, but she could see that sometimes it might be necessary. It was different for Blodeuwedd, even her treachery had been part of the cycle of the land—the king had to die in order to be born again,

fibre fills, protects,
feeding Lepidoptera,
earth-sweet nourishment

soothe coughs, calm breathing,
flush away swelling and pain,
suckle and sedate.

but at least Blodeuwedd had not remained passive. She looked around the assembly, still cheering, full of good food and now satiated with story. They would refill glasses, break into clusters, chatting and amiable, assemble again in the field for the ceremony and to toast the turning of the longest day. She wished Deniel had been able to stay for all of it. She turned towards the sound of her name and Émilie reached out a hand to rest it briefly on her arm. There's something I need to tell you, she said.

Émilie drew Viola outside. She'd watched the sun getting lower, uncertain how long to wait before creeping into the cottage. It was deep dusk before she ventured in, another twenty minutes and the sky would be dark and, on the other side of the hamlet, everyone would be in the gather-hall for the story-telling. She turned the door handle slowly so that it would make no noise. In the downstairs room everything was tranquil, the embers of a fire glowing in the stove that was both heating and cooking for the cottage. She stood

tap root to anchor,
sucking out water reserves,
root fibres to feed.

blood soothing berries,
scarlet for immunity,
the heart relaxes

listening. No sound. She crept up the steep staircase that opened into the bedroom above. Beneath the bedcover, Deniel had curled into himself, foetal. She drew closer and a tremor went though him. Deniel! Deniel, can you hear me? A ragged breath, hardly audible even as she put her face close to his. Beth. Did he say Beth, or was it just the last air leaving his body? Yes, Deniel, it's Beth. I'm here. She took his hand, clammy and curled into a fist that she gently undid to rest in her own. I'm here, Deniel, Beth's here. There was no response but as she lent in to see if there was still breath, a convulsion shook him, then a sound she had heard too many times before. Silence. She laid her hand over his heart. Nothing. She put her face close to his. Nothing. It was over. She scanned the room. The bed clothes seemed hardly disturbed by his slight weight. There was no vomit. A tray lay on the floor next to the bed. A kettle stood on a trivet on the wooden chest next to the bed, beside it a mug that was no doubt Christophe's work. She sniffed the residue

deep rooted, spreading
wide as veins and arteries,
to tender the heart.

145

nettle, oak, primrose,
bean, broom, meadowsweet burdock,
chestnut and hawthorn.

of the liquid and lifted the kettle lid to peer into the mash
of needles and seeds. He must have taken a huge dose for his
heart to stop so suddenly. She hoped he had thought that
Beth was with him in those last seconds. She stroked a lock
of damp hair from his forehead, closed his eyes, her hand
resting on his face for a few moments. Enough, she said to
the little room, rising, placing the mug and kettle on the
tray, picking it up and carrying it downstairs. It was dusk
now and she searched the cottage's cupboards for a candle
torch, lighting it from the embers of the fire. She walked to
L'Autre Rive slowly. She hadn't eaten or drunk for hours and
had spent most of the day uncomfortable and tense. She
could feel the energy draining from her, but she was relieved
that Viola was at the back of the hall. There's something I
need to tell you, she said, drawing Viola into the still-warm
air of the night.

nettle, oak, primrose,
bean, meadowsweet, broom. burdock,
chestnut, hawthorn roots.

worms and foxes heard our weeping—great guttural sobs
of tree and plant, root and mycelia, screech-panic
juddering through howling bodies of stem and trunk into
badger and crow, ant, swallow and deer, while two-

Chapter 12

She heard herself weeping, great guttural sobs and then
Catherine was in the doorway asking Émilie a hundred
questions and Émilie was rocking her, telling Catherine that
they should get her into L'Autre Rive. They manoeuvred her
onto the old sofa in the big downstairs room, Émilie asking
Catherine to find find Lisette, find Isabelle, not to alert
anyone else. She'd explain everything soon, she heard Émilie
say to Catherine, and then it was just the two of them for a
few minutes, Émilie stroking her hair, cradling her and still
she could hear those inhuman howls that she slowly
understood were coming from herself, trying to choke them
back as Lisette and Isabelle entered. Mum! Mum! She
breathed deeply. Lisette hardly ever called her Mum. Isabelle
sat next to her, on her other side Émilie moved to make
space for Lisette, Catherine watching them all. She couldn't
tell how long it was before her heaving sobs subsided. They

cells of mycelia no longer bringing news of famine or
feast, health or disease, in the worst of times no news to
proclaim for roots were cut, wrenched into air, while we
were riven, wounded darkness torn open, severed fibres

stayed with her, asked nothing, let the wailing take its time.
When she was quieter, only occasional gulps of tears racking
her body, Émilie told the story again, a shorter version this
time, enough for them to realise that Deniel was gone, that
he'd taken yew poison, that he was at peace. Catherine
nodded. How did you know? I can't really explain. We
exchanged a few words. There was something about the way
his posture changed for a moment, and something he said—
just a word—like he'd made a decision and knew it was
right. All I can say is that something passed between us. I
knew I had to be there for him today and that if I spoke to
anyone I'd loose my resolve to simply walk beside him. Yes,
she heard Catherine say. I can see that. Yes, she heard herself
echo faintly. Lisette hugged her tightly. Do we tell people
before or after the ceremony? Her voice sounded distant.
And Alex and Gaëlle-Anne? Surely they should know
straight away? She looked towards Isabelle, who looked
paler than the Winter moon, but nodded. Yes, immediately,

roots were cut, the mycelia riven, roots wrenched into air, our wounded darkness torn open, severed fibres spilled, veil of earth rent asunder cutting off signals, starving of nutrients, contact, leaving the dying screaming alone,

Isabelle agreed, and it's they who should decide when to tell everyone else. Strains of violin music and clapping swelled as Catherine opened the door to go and find Alex and Gaëlle-Anne, incongruous, jarring. She wanted to shout at Gwilherm to have more respect, but he and Zoé, Pierrick on guitar, the dancers and those clapping along, none of them had any idea that the world had just changed. Perhaps Alex and Gaëlle-Anne were spinning one another in circles under the Summer stars while Deniel lay cold and slowly stiffening. Of course, when they came into the building, it was obvious that they knew instantly. Why else would those inside be slumped together, tear-stained and pallid, tense with news? They cried softly together, a different kind of dance, asked quiet questions, nodded. So dignified and brave, she thought. The boys are already asleep in your spare room, Gaëlle-Anne said at last. I don't think we should wake them, and Pascal and Armel are with them too. It would be too much to... Yes, she agreed. Let them sleep. What we

creatures of soil slaughtered and squashed, rich humus rammed closed, oxygen-choked, watertight-dense and ungiving, scarred battle ground dead, tree limbs torn and left in ravaged mud, plant bodies tossed on desecrated

wondered… We weren't sure whether you'd want to tell everyone tonight—before the ceremony or afterwards… She watched them exchange a glance. Before, Alex said. I mean if you and Isabelle can… it would be good to say something during the rite—thank the stars, the world, the earth for him, wish him peace with my mother… I'm not sure what I'm saying exactly, but if you could… Of course, she said. Absolutely, Isabelle added. She felt a movement at her side and Lisette was asking Émilie if she was alright. I'm a little… perhaps a little faint. Lisette rose to make tea, despatching Catherine to find food. How calm and efficient her daughter was. Lemon balm, meadowsweet and rose, Lisette said, when she returned with a large tray bearing a pot and several cups. We could all do with some of this. She watched Catherine put food in front of her friend, but she didn't fuss or insist. She watched Alex and Gaëlle-Anne leaning on each other. They looked exhausted but they were holding one another together, would do their grieving together later, again in the morning when Fragan realised that Deniel was not there, again when they told their children… Quietly, they discussed how they wanted to make the announcement, then Lisette left to ask Zoé, Pierrick and Alice to help her let everyone know that they should meet in the gather-hall, that there was something Viola and Isabelle needed to say…

Isabelle stood at the front of the hall, she would need to raise her voice, she knew, aware that it was thinner in the last few years, sometimes felt as though it didn't reach much further than the person standing next to her, but the silence in the barn let her know that they were listening, and Viola was at her side. She counted each birthday now as a surprise gift and today's had been one of the most memorable—the intensity as she'd read tarot cards for Catherine to ease her worry for Émilie, the thoughtful gifts—the unexpected and precious scarf from Gwilherm, a beautiful note book that Lisette had made for her, new crayons from Viola, herbal pigments worked into the wax—the song Lisette had composed for her mother, still reverberating in her mind, and her last brief but emotional farewell with Deniel… Deniel, she needed to tell them about… She felt a wave of heat prickle through her, remembering the insufferably humid July day when Deniel and Alex had posted a notice on their door to say that Beth had died. She had feared for both of them, not only because it was clear to everyone that neither of them expected to survive Beth by many days, but because, if they did, she could imagine one of them might take his own life without Beth there. But they lived and they supported each other, Alex changing from a prickly young man to a kind and skilful member of the community, as devoted to Deniel as Deniel was to him, both of them eventually benefitting so much from Gaëlle-Anne's quiet strength and patience. Deniel was many things to this village, she heard herself saying, but above all he was a husband, father, grandfather and beloved friend. We all

slicing ancient heartwood uprooting and mauling,
wreaking holocaust on canopy and understorey as, fewer,
we huddled, bereaved, unable to shade the drying earth,
unable to make enough rain, unable to forest the world,

knew that his time with us was running out, but we hadn't foreseen how quickly or the decision he would take. What I know for certain is that he was a brave man, who thought deeply about everything he did. The gap he leaves will be enormous for all of us, but especially for Alex, Gaëlle-Anne, and their boys, who won't hear about this loss until they wake, and then their parents want to be there for them first. All our thoughts are with Deniel's family, with whatever they need from us… She felt so old, so inadequate to this task, so desperate not to say something clichéd, not to miss saying something necessary… She glanced towards Alex and Gaëlle-Anne and…

Alex stepped forward. He felt the whole assembly leaning towards him, as though they could take his weight. I haven't begun to make sense of the news you've just heard, he told them. Like Isabelle said, we knew we were losing Deniel, but on some level we didn't believe it, even on the days when he was obviously trying to hide the pain. I hope, when we…

clawing and tearing, pulsing horror on horror, smashing
each resurrection, but still we rebirthed beneath the sick
and surviving, new planted and unkinned, in bad soil and
dry soil, acid earth and traumatised land, beneath the

when we have a ceremony to say goodbye... that... that I'll have something coherent to say... probably not something that will do justice to that long ago philosophy degree I can hardly remember taking... He was relieved that there was a trickle of soft laughter to puncture the ache in his chest. But for now, I just want to say thank you to all of you, for listening to Isabelle, and to Isabelle for doing this, and Viola for caring for the man who became my father... he trailed away. Were there people who could say great and moving things at such moments? People were surrounding him, patting an arm, embracing him, wishing him and his family well, anything they could do... just ask... He found himself nodding, longing to be only with Gaëlle-Anne and she was there, at his side, leading him out into the mild air of midsummer night, plucking one of the waiting candle torches from those ranged around ready to be carried to one of twelve homes. He thought of saying something about the boys, but knew they were safe and asleep, that they'd be back

thinned remnants of forest that should be world, knowing
they would come no matter our howling, waiting to face
massacre the next day or the next...
until, cut down themselves, they ceased....

in the morning before Ronan and Paol woke, and he needed
to fall into his bed, maybe to sleep or, if it would not come,
at least to let the first tears flow, knowing it would all be
there to face the next day and the next...

their howling, knowing how kith and kin trembled,
waiting for massacre the next day or the next... yet still
we rebuilt, below as above, connecting again...
until, one day, howling their own grief, they ceased....

and when the breath won't come—
in congestion, asthma, sorrow,
and when catarrh or gloom won't flow away
or rage or fever burn,

Chapter 13

Isabelle was up early. Their friends would gather again today, to clear and clean, to set everything back ready for the days when the daylight would incrementally shrink until they reached the shortest day and began the climb again back towards the light. It felt apt that today there was just a little less light than the previous one. She made a large pot of tea, anticipating others rising or arriving soon and Lisette was in the kitchen before the herbs had finished steeping. I thought we should be early in case Ronan or Paol wake, she said. Yes, Isabelle agreed, though the young ones were all so exhausted when they went to bed. I always think they look like puppies—curled around each other and completely in their dreams. They're going to miss Deniel so much. Lisette hugged her. We all are, but his family… it's so hard to make sense of death. I mean, we know it's there, but when it happens… it feels bizarre that someone can be there and

in the rich loam of the underland they have always buried
what is precious—bodies, ashes, bones, sacred art, the
prints of their souls as hands, images of their
metamorphoses and stories, treasures, tools and food for

and when the lymph is stuck
in deafness or in mourning,
and infections flare or emotions flame
and a cooling touch is needed,

then not be. They poured mugs of the Summertea that she
and Viola had blended yesterday—packed with Solstice
flowers—chamomile, calendula, elderflower, fennel,
lavender, peppermint, lemon balm, hibiscus, St John's wort,
sprinkled with generous handfuls of rose and violet petals. It
tasted of sun and health, of days blossoming and light. We
need this today, Isabelle said, savouring the tang of the
hibiscus that balanced the mints and aromatics. Should I
take a cup to Viola? Lisette asked after they'd sat in silence
for a while, herself thinking about how much she would
miss Deniel's solid and quiet presence, what it must have
been like to make that decision, to be so alone with it. She
was grateful that Émilie had been with him at the end, that
she had told him that she was Beth. She realised she hadn't
answered Lisette's question. I thought she'd be up before
both of us, Isabelle responded. I wasn't sure she'd sleep at all,
but perhaps the distress exhausted her. She put down her
mug. Maybe we should let her sleep on if she needs it.

the apocalypse, refuged far below our roots or carved as
meaning into rock, as we too commit our dead to decay
into new life in the earth, wood and leaf, stem and flower,
microbes and every creature that moves, transforming to

when waters burn within or tears scald without,
when head or heart writhe in bitter pain,
and the gut is sour or feelings acrimonious,
when insomnia taunts or loss oppresses,

Lisette sucked in her lip. Yes. And Gwilherm? Isabelle waved a hand towards the cracked hard standing at the front of the house—He decided to sleep in his wagon. He'll probably make tea in there when he surfaces. She watched Lisette forming a question, deciding not to ask it, then thinking again. There's something on your mind? she prompted. Viola, Lisette said simply. You know I said I thought she was worrying about something, seemed more… inside herself, more than usual… It's just that yesterday, while everyone was arriving—I was talking to Alice and… Can I show you something? She stood up. Of course, Isabelle said, watching Lisette scurry to the sitting area and reappear with the tarot. Lisette worked through the cards to one she already knew the location of. She picked it out quickly and laid it face down, then searched for another—the queen of cups. Viola's card, Isabelle said. Oisín didn't only foresee what she looked like, it has her spirit too—a woman of generosity and inspiration. Lisette traced the figure with a finger tip.

humus, becoming rock over aeons, deep in our transforming bodies, under loam and roots, beneath our networks of food communication, into this sanctuary of roots, mycelia, rock, what is beloved is delivered to the

when digestion curdles
or bereavement haunts,
memory fails or anxiety gnaws,
and when cysts swell or anger erupts,

Sometimes to the point of self-sacrifice, she said. Yes, Isabelle agreed. So often our strengths and weaknesses are different sides of one another. And a healer too, a problem solver. Empathy can be hard to keep in check sometimes. Lisette lifted the other card she had chosen and turned it over. Isabelle smiled. Ah, so you have solved the riddle. She watched Lisette chewing over responses. It's weird, but it's never even occurred to me before that the king to Viola's queen isn't my father. But Hugo must have seen this, he wouldn't have been so... so obtuse. Isabelle put a hand on Lisette's arm. You're not obtuse, anything but. Sometimes we see what is needful for the time. Viola adored Hugo but Hugo knew they didn't have all the time in the world together. That lip-biting again. But has Viola seen it? I mean, she must have, but when? Do you think she might not have noticed for a while, it seems... She trailed away and Isabelle gave her arm a squeeze. I'm fairly certain that she remained oblivious for a long time. What I'm not

earth, what is treasured relinquished, placed among us to become holy as land, in letting go they yield ancestors and what they have held dear to become as mysterious as we are to them. here too, they place their waste, the toxins

the chest inflames, melancholia overwhelms,
when children cough unable to rest,
or any sink in grim depression,
and when tumours prey or distress torments,

certain of is what she is making of it now. Lisette stood and
filled a plate with leftovers, offered it to Isabelle, who shook
her head. Her appetite, which had always been good, had
diminished a little recently, she realised. Lisette bit into a
slice of cold chicken and sourdough and chewed slowly.
Isabelle watched her processing, the food giving her respite
from the hundred questions assailing her. It feels like
destiny, Lisette said at last. And I don't like the thought of
that—that we're just playing a part that has been set out for
us. Isabelle put her hands together, fingertips touching, a
gesture that Hugo had often used, she realised. Not destiny,
she told Lisette, more… possibility. When we do a reading,
we never tell someone that it's their future, do we? The cards
hold up a mirror to what might be happening, to directions
we might go in or might welcome being warned not to go
in. I think the images offer the same—a snapshot of the
possible. The people on each card always have something of
the character of that card, but they can also change. How

and spoils that will not decay, matter with half lives
longer than our deepest memories, older than forest,
destructive as stars, substances tortured from fossilised
bodies to become waste that chokes fish in oceans,

would you feel if…

Gwilherm stood in the doorway, they had not heard him come in and he coughed slightly, uneasy that they might think he was eavesdropping. Gwilherm, good morning. Isabelle greeted him, waving him to sit at the table. Tea? He nodded, but didn't sit. Thank you. I thought I might take it back to the vardo if… He glanced at Lisette, sure he was making a mess of this. Of course, Isabelle, said. She got up and came back with their largest mug. I didn't think anyone would be up and about yet, he said. Isabelle's smile, what was she thinking, he wondered. Lisette looked from one to the other of them. Astute girl, Gwilherm told himself. Maybe I should take a drink to Viola, Lisette said. Gwilherm almost blurted 'no!' but Isabelle was quicker. Let me, she said, pouring a small cup and heading for the stairs. Gwilherm picked up the large mug. I'll see you in a bit, he said to Lisette. I expect Alex and Gaëlle-Anne will be here soon. He stood a moment longer, feeling awkward, then

there is cool, sweet, balm of grounding violet.

turned and left with the tea. He kept his eyes on the vardo, sure that Lisette was watching him, perhaps Isabelle too from Viola's window, her bedroom empty, as Isabelle had surely guessed.

ourselves, for the canker buried in our life-giving underland, but still we persist, still there is the tough, spreading root of cool, sweet, balming, grounding violet.

flowers of imbolc,
we appear, the cycle turns,
ah, snowdrops return

Chapter 14

She watched Gwilherm pour the tea into two smaller mugs.
Isabelle or Lisette? she asked. Isabelle, he told her. I felt like
a five year old. She sipped the tea. I'm sorry. I'm… She
choked back tears, wondering how many more there could
possibly be. She'd held herself together for a little while as
Isabelle and Alex told the community about Deniel, then
left Isabelle and Lisette to be alone, to sob as quietly as she
could manage, before lying in bed, sleepless and nauseous,
going over images of Deniel taking the yew poison. Émilie
had said he hadn't vomited, that there was only one
convulsion near the end, but still… She must have fallen
into shallow sleep for a while. She came round to images of
Hugo, sick and feverish, still holding her hand as though he
was the one caring for her, confused with Deniel, calling for
Beth, reaching out… She'd surfaced restless, got up, hardly
aware that she walking to the vardo. No apologies needed,

our memories reach
deeper than oceans, our roots
hold fast shifting earth.

Gwilherm said, handing her a cup. I'm glad you felt… She smiled. Lisette will tell you my greatest talents are oblivion and distance, she said. It's odd—I have a lot of empathy when I'm working with someone alongside the herbs, but I don't give much of myself away I suppose. He put down his tea and held her gaze. Do you know why that is? She considered. Lots of theories, but I think partly just Reagh. It was a magical place, a maze big enough to feature on GoogleEarth when we had such things, a Druid grove and a faery ring and a river, all in the garden. Life there was very quiet and I spent a lot of time with Sarah, my grandmother. Saoirse and Faolán loved me, there was never any doubt of that, but they adored each other and were committed to their art. Faolán was a sculptor, would sometimes be away for months if he was working on some huge project. Saoirse painted—extraordinary abstracts that somehow had landscapes in them, but you had to let yourself fall into the piece to see the patterns. I was their darling but not their

we are sweet, cool, moist,
violet spring—prophetic
dreams to soothe all grief.

focus. I don't mean that critically—they had real vocations. I developed a strong interior world, a kind of self-sufficiency. I was fascinated by other people but reticent to open up to them. Does that make sense? He nodded slowly. It does. My mother was an artist too. It makes a lot of sense. Really? Tell me about her. She had just said more about herself than she had said to anyone since Hugo died. She needed a pause, but she also wanted to know more about him.

Gwilherm took another mouthful of tea. Part of him wanted to say that he was as unused as she was to talking about himself. When he'd been with Caroline he had told her very little, but that was never going to be a relationship. He had a chance of something different with Viola, but felt out of his depth. Still… She was called Flóra, he told her. She came from Pecs in Hungary and moved to Budapest to study. She did an exchange programme in Paris during her art degree and was fascinated by a Lebanese artist who lived

Cradling safe the roots
of bright Spring, clivers, nettles,
to enliven, cleanse

between Paris and a commune in Brittany, Erquy. For her project that Summer she went to paint in this little coastal place that inspired the artist, and also managed to get an interview with her. She was called Etel Adnan, and was also a poet and philosopher. And that was where she met my father, Yann. He looked up and saw how intently she was listening. And they stayed in Brittany? she asked. They moved to Landivisiau in Finistère when I was four and later to Quimper. My mother found a small gallery there. It had studio space but also a shopfront—she sold her work, and work of other artists too. He'd left to go to university in the Autumn of 2045 and often asked himself why he'd returned to Quimper after a degree in music and composition. He composed in the evenings after working long days as a barista, though he'd planned to go back to Paris and take a masters degree, something that would never happen. When the… he hesitated and she reached a hand towards him. He had held her all night, let her sob, then sleep, her head on

yellow candles hedge
ditches in agrimony
sun on a grey day

his chest becoming heavy, but he hadn't wanted to disturb
her. Why was he so reticent to tell her about his life? When
the Bane came, he said, both my parents died early. My
father... my father got sick and my mother... He took a
deep breath. She didn't want to live without him, she...
Viola moved closer to him and put an arm around him. She
killed herself? He nodded. So I understand what you mean
about your parents being devoted to each other, except, it
wasn't really devotion with them... he caught the abrasive
note in his voice and breathed deeply. I think I'm still angry
with her, he admitted. At the time I felt her suicide was
weakness, an over-dependency on my father, a refusal to be
in a world that wasn't full of middle-class privilege... But
what I really felt is that she didn't love me enough to stay
alive with me and I suppose the rage was just a cover for this
awful grief... I'm not putting this very well. She leaned in
closer. I think you are, she said softly. Do you want to stop?
He was surprised that he didn't want to call a halt to the tale.

high Summer and roots
meander, unfurl and spread,
each day new fungi.

He'd heard people telling their stories, some had a way of making their trauma special, more significant than anything others had endured. He didn't want to be one of those, but Viola was opening a space. He felt himself back in Quimper in a way he hadn't allowed in over a decade. In the early days of the Shift he'd realised that this wasn't just a temporary economic crisis after the horrors of the Bane. He'd bought up as many supplies as possible, going to different supermarkets and DIY stores in rotation, using cash. There were large basement rooms under his mother's gallery and she'd had the walls dry-lined so she could store artworks. As things worsened, he stashed his parents van in the garage behind the gallery and removed the distributor cap and spark plugs so no-one would steal it. He stored petrol in one of the basement rooms and brought some comforts into another—a mattress and blankets, a portable gas stove, a few EverLights, pots, crockery and clothes. When the looting and violence began he stopped going out. The farthest he

path strewn with branches,
twigs, leaves, fallen in high winds,
Summer bows to Fall

ventured was to empty the foul but lidded bucket into the toilet on the half landing of the stone staircase that led from the basement to the studio. This he'd allowed himself every other day at most. When he emerged, pale and thin, he found that there were things that had not been taken from the surrounding shops and houses—strings for musical instruments, some art supplies, books. His searches were cautious, but occasionally he found soap or candles, left behind cooking pots and utensils, once a long length of rope, but Quimper was not deserted and every trip might be his last. He began filling the van on a moonless and cloudy night and set off with no direction in mind, heading inland. He drove at night, siphoning remnants of fuel from abandoned cars, doing only a few miles and collecting anything that might be useful in any abandoned building he came across. He stayed for a while in a remote house where the people had died and there were remnants of food— the tinned goods still edible, some bags of pasta and dried

and while berries plump,
roots will fatten, nutrition
swelling with Autumn.

beans, but he knew he would need others if he was going to survive. When he arrived in the small hamlet of La Gare it had seemed deserted. The houses were spread out and some were empty, but seven families remained and they were glad to have him amongst them. He'd set up home in an old tourist gite in what had once been a railway station. He used the upstairs spaces for storage and made a home on the ground floor. For as long as he could find fuel and syphon it off, he had used the van for his foraging, making trips to Morlaix and Brest, but they were dangerous and desolate places. He did better exploring deserted hamlets, lone houses or trading things between the small settlements that were springing up. He paused and finished his tea. And the vardo? Viola asked. They used to belong to a tourist company, he said. People used to hire them in Locmaria-Berrien. The owners would set them up with a carthorse and they'd trundle through the forest down the old railway track that had become a trail for hikers and cyclists. There were

haws, hips, seeds, berries,
fruits of the ripening world,
to survive Winter.

two wagons abandoned near Gite d'étape and he'd adopted
and restored them. The horses' descendants had become
part of the community and they were happy for him to use
them to bring supplies they couldn't grow themselves,
foraging finds and things that others made that they didn't
have the skills for themselves. Sometimes he'd be away for a
month or longer, sometimes only a couple of weeks. He'd
developed a few circuits and got to know other foragers,
swapping items or crops with them, occasionally passing on
letters and messages to people in places that had once
seemed not that far away, where loved ones may or may not
still live. Sometimes responses were passed back for him to
deliver, something which made him feel the world was a
shade more beautiful. He felt more drained than his cup and
rested his head against Viola. So that's me, he said. Thank
you, she replied. And thank you for last night. And a
question. He lifted his head and looked into her eyes. When
I showed you some of my favourites from the tarot

as the seasons cool,
roots warm, feed—ginger, burdock,
riches for dark days.

yesterday, I think you noticed that there was one I held back? He nodded. I'd like to show it to you if you want to see it. He stood. I do, he said, though I suspect we will have some explaining to do to Lisette and Isabelle.

Isabelle watched Gwilherm and Viola emerge from the wagon. Alex and Gaëlle-Anne had just left and she'd told them that Viola was still sleeping, that she'd had a bad night. They'd understood. They looked exhausted and she and Lisette had left them alone with the boys while they told them, as gently as possible, about their grandfather. Lisette had taken a picnic breakfast upstairs for Armel and Pascal once Alex and his family had left, and then walked both boys home, though Armel had been adamant that he didn't need to be walked with. She smiled as the door opened, walked towards Viola and took her in her arms. Sit down, sit, both of you. I'm going to make breakfast and you are both going to eat it. They sat obediently. The tarot, tidied into its box, was still on the table and she noticed Viola open

bright holly on snow,
mistletoe above ivy,
Winter's last berry,

it and begin looking for a card. They are together at the bottom, she said, setting a kettle on the stove, cracking eggs into a pan. Viola looked up and smiled. Thank you. She placed the queen of cups in front of Gwilherm. This one you know from yesterday, she said. And this one—she put the king of cups next to his queen. And this one is Sir Bedivere, she said, also known as… Isabelle watched Gwilherm pick up the card, gaze at Viola and then look towards her. Is it really…? His voice was a whisper. It is, Isabelle answered for them—but, as I was saying to Lisette, the cards always hold out no more than possibility. He studied the card again. What sort of person is the king of cups? he asked. Someone rather like you, Isabelle hoped the laughter in her voice would be taken for warmth. She tipped the scrambled eggs onto slices of sourdough and set them on the table, picking up the box with the remaining cards. Someone who is patient, kind and loyal, she said, leafing though the cards till she found the one she wanted, someone who I believe will

some will hibernate,
some draw within, surviving
on what is stored deep.

be a good father to this beautiful girl. She placed the page of cups card on the table—a girl a little younger than Lisette offering a ceramic chalice that overflowed with golden liquid, around her, in a forest clearing, flowers of every colour in bloom. She comes with so much promise, Isabelle said. Healing for the past, hope for the future. Flóra, she added. I believe her name will be Flóra.

Acknowledgements

Each day while I was writing the first draft of the stories of leaves/branches/flowers/seeds and of roots and mycelia (the panels which appear at the top and bottom of the chapters), I walked for at least an hour, usually longer, in the forest that surrounds my home, part of what is left of the ancient forest of Huelgoat. My aim was simply to soak up the atmosphere and pay attention. Every day I returned knowing what should go into the next chapter. My thanks to the forest for helping me to listen.

Jn Chapter 4, the lines in italics and the line 'every atom belonging to me as good belongs to you', which is included in the sound waves of the leaves and flowers, are taken from Walt Whitman, *The Leaves of Grass*.

The names of extinct trees in the list of the dead (Chapter 5), began as a list of all the trees and plants that have become extinct since 2010 plus all the trees that are currently endangered or have critical status (https://www.unep.org/resources/report/world-list-threatened-trees). But before finishing the list of species beginning with 'A' that fit into these groups, I had filled enough space to complete the 'roots' section of the rest of the book. This was sobering. The names finally included are of the most endangered trees and plants in Europe as of 2023. Since the book is set in 2065, I have made the leap to listing these as 'extinct' in the time of the novel. This list is not comprehensive, however, even for this limited group. The EU Red List considers that 42% of European trees are critical, endangered or vulnerable and The International Union for the Conservation of Nature considers that 58% of trees face extinction in the next decades, with trees such as elm, ash, horse chestnut and rowan under threat.

The paper 'How do plants feel the heat and survive?' by Anthony Guihur, Matthieu E Rebeaud and Pierre Goloubinoff, was helpful in thinking about the plants' word choices for feelings in response to heat and drought in Chapter 6 (https://doi.org/10.1016/j.tibs.2022.05.004 A)

A paper by Hiroyuki Takamoto, 'Acquisition of terrestrial life by human ancestors influenced by forest microclimate', provided the idea used in Chapter 8, that human evolution began in forests not savannah (https://www.nature.com/articles/s41598-017-05942-5)

Other papers support the idea that bipedalism also began in trees—for example: 'Wild chimpanzee behavior suggests that a savanna-mosaic habitat did not support the emergence of hominin terrestrial bipedalism'. (https://www.science.org/)

Forests, specifically rain forests, may also be at the root of the evolution of *Homo sapiens'* cultural and physical diversity since populations isolated in these dense areas contributed to the evolution of our biological malleability and cultural adaptability, as argued by Eleanor Scerri in 'Human evolution: secrets of early ancestors could be unlocked by African rainforests'. (https://theconversation.com/human-evolution-secrets-of-early-ancestors-could-be-unlocked-by-african-rainforests-101636)

The quote used in the leaf story of Chapter 9, 'to breathe the linden tree when it is a volcano of bees', is from Sidonie-Gabrielle Colette.

In the same chapter, the leaf story on p.119 is paraphrased from a French fairy tale, *Le Prince Lutin*, written in 1697 by Marie Catherine d'Aulnoy. Lutins are pixies or sprites, one of many species of fairy folk in Breton legend, along with korrigans, siren-like little people who live near water, and polpegan who, like the Irish púca, are shape-shifting creatures who can be either benevolent or malevolent.

Trees breathe out fungal spores and particles that make rain, yet when the rain falls on them they exhibit a panic-like response since the droplets can contain bacteria and pathogens and their panic communicates to other trees to turn on defence mechanisms. This is referenced in Chapter 10 in the haiku on p.129. (https://www.sci.news/biology/plants-reaction-rain-panic-07749.html).

I have lost count of the books I have read about forests and the plants that grow there, but would particularly recommend those by David George Haskell (particularly *The Songs of Trees* & *Thirteen Ways to Smell a Tree*); Peter Wohlleben (particularly *The Power of Trees*); Suzanne Simard (*Finding the Mother Tree*) and Robin Wall Kimmerer (*Braiding Sweetgrass*).

My list of personal thanks is endless. I'm constantly grateful to the poets and prose writers I mentor and the community of writers who attend my workshops, read my blogs and send comments in the Kith Community. I learn so much from teaching and working with others. Similarly, working as an editor for poets and prose writers is a privilege that immerses me in language and imagination.

I'm blessed to be accompanied on my own healing journey by amazing, gifted and generous yoga nidrā mentors. Huge thanks to Yoli Maya Yeh Joseph for the spaces she holds and for the openness and wisdom of those in her community. And thanks to Uma Dinsmore-Tuli for her circles of community and rest.

I'm fortunate to be learning herbalism at The Plant Medicine School and thankful to the tutors, clinic supervisors and my peers for so much shared knowledge combined with heart and intuition. A special thanks to my study group of green goddesses, Annette, Aoife, Carole and Izabela.

I've been lucky to find myself in inspiring spaces to write this book. Huge thanks to Sophia in Budapest; James, Evie and Merrily for sharing Reagh in Roscommon (again); to Daniel & Ross and to Caroline for their wonderful havens in Cornwall.

Thanks to Adam Craig for listening to early drafts read aloud and designing the exquisite cover, and to John Barnie for meticulous copy editing. Thanks to Catherine Coldstream, Uma Dinsmore-Tuli, Susan Richardson and Yoli Maya Yeh Joseph for reading the manuscript and for their generous comments.

A special thanks to Tamsyn and Finn for discovering the real L'Autre Rive, the unique and welcoming space of café and bookshop nestled in the forest, which inspired the setting for this novel.

Above all, thanks to my family, whose love, conversations and support make all the difference every day.

Author biography

Jan Fortune is a herbalist, yoga nidrā practitioner, writer, editor and mentor for poets and prose writers. She runs the writing community 'Kith' (https://janfortune.com/) and the herb-centred healing space, 'Triskelewell' (https://triskelewell.com/), which has a home on Mighty Networks as 'Herbal healing with Triskelewell' (https://herbal-healing-with-triskelewell.mn.co/about). She also publishes regular newsletters and podcasts on Substack (https://alchemicalwonderings.substack.com/) where she writes at the intersection of story, poetry, herbalism and alchemy.

Jan lives with her husband and son in a hamlet in a forest, and also has three daughters and a son-in-law, daughter-in-law and two grandchildren.

Her previous novels include The Standing Ground trilogy (*The Standing Ground, The Roots of the Ground, The Messenger of the Ground*), The Casilda trilogy (*This is the End of the Story, A Remedy for All Things, For Hope is Always Born*) and *Saoirse's Crossing*. Her prose poetry collection is *Stale Bread & Miracles* and her most recent poetry collection is *at world's end, begin*.

Milton Keynes UK
Ingram Content Group UK Ltd.
UKHW020917230524
443054UK00008B/76